Twisted Tales of the Heart

Printed in the United States of America

Cover Design: SheerGenious

Editing: LPW Editing & Consulting, LLC www.litapward.com

First Printing, 2020
ISBN – 13: 978-1-7343853-2-8

ISBN – 10:

Books by Yolanda

For Teens:

Harriet High Series

Mysteries of Harriet High: "The Secret of Twila Anderson"

Twila's Dilemma: Field of Lies; Touchdown in Truth

Mommy's Girl

Summer Rain

For Adults:

Wolf in Sheep's Clothing

Eyes of the Enemy

Twisted Tales of the Heart

Yolanda Randolph

TABLE OF CONTENTS

Twisted Tales of the Heart

AMANDA

1

O ne hundred dollars a month! What am I supposed to do with that?!" Amanda Ingram yelled at the top of her lungs.

"Ms. Ingram, one more outburst from you and I will hold you in contempt," the bald, heavy-set judge warned.

Amanda glanced over at James, her six-year-old son's father. "I hate him; I don't know what I ever saw in him," she uttered.

"Ms. Ingram? Do you agree with the terms?"

Confused, Amanda looked up at the judge. "I'm sorry Your Honor. What was the question?"

"Ms. Ingram, I had about enough of you," the judge scolded.

Ignoring the snickering in the background, Amanda focused her attention on the judge.

"I asked you about the amount of the child support. Do you agree with everything discussed today?"

Cutting her eye over at James and his girlfriend of the month, she cringed at the smirk on his face. *Why? It doesn't matter if I agree. His stingy butt ain't trying to give anything extra. A continuance is what I'll have to deal with if I say no. Then, we won't get anything at all for the next few months. Damn it, I do need the money and his lousy one hundred dollars could at least get a few things.* "Yes, Your Honor. I will make do with what was offered.

"Good, you're both free to go. Have a lovely day. Case dismissed!" the judge blurted before hitting his gavel.

"What a waste," Amanda mumbled before storming out of the courtroom.

"Yo, Amanda! Aye! Wait up!"

Amanda sighed, rolled her eyes, and turned towards the man she despised. "What is it, James?" she asked in an irritated tone.

"Damn, hello to you too."

Sucking her teeth, Amanda turned to walk away.

"I was hoping to see my son this weekend."

Turning back, she stared at James for a few seconds. "Uh, Dylan has been asking for you for months and now you want to all of a sudden, just like that, see him now?"

"Yeah, just like that. I am his father and I have my rights. Just because I don't want you doesn't mean that I don't want to be with my son."

Amanda chuckled before responding. "You have a right to see your son. Ain't that some shit. Well James, you are not

4

welcomed at my house and I'm not letting him go to yours so he can be around whoever the hoe of the month is for this month."

"You mean for the week," James laughed a menacing laugh and winked at Amanda. "I switched my game up since I had you so…"

"You are one crazy ass dude. I don't know why I got hooked up with you in the first place."

"The stallion; gets ya'll every time. I shouldn't have never let you touch it first. No judgment, you ain't the first one to get all over yourself when you saw my stallion. That one over there is just as stupid as you were over it."

"Ugh, get over yourself! You ain't all that. You know why I don't want you up in my house."

"Oh, damn, you still trippin'? Okay, I see how you want to do this."

Amanda shook her head. "Why are you surprised James? You should know how I feel about you stepping foot into my house. You used to have all those trashy whores in there; messing up all my sheets."

"Aww, you still hurt about that. Come on, that was years ago, and I bought you some new sheets so you should be all over all that by now."

Amanda stared blank-faced at her son's father, not sure how to approach him or his mouth, she knows how he is; he's been this way since they met. She used to think it was a turn on but now, all she wanted to do was punch him every time she saw him.

"I tell you what. How about if I come over tonight and make things right between us? I can do you in the same places I've done the others."

Amanda glared at James. "I should smack that nasty, stupid ass grin off your face you sick bast—"

"Shhh, just chill. We are right here in the courthouse, Mandy. You smack me and you will go straight downstairs, to the right, and off to the left. I been there a few times and you won't like it. They got different kind of chicks in jail and you ain't ready for that."

"Whateva and don't call me Mandy!" Feeling a bit hot, she looked around, hoping that people would continue to mind their own business. To her relief, they were. This was a Thursday, rainy afternoon, in the busiest courthouse in Baltimore so there was lots of commotion going on all at once. Some had frowns on their faces; or rather focused looks and others, who just came out of child support court, wore happy smiles and looks of content. Well, with the exception of one woman who was pushing two kids in a double stroller and pulling one by the hand, all three-toddler aged. She looked like the world was all on her shoulders and she was looking for some relief... any kind.

"What's going on here? What's the problem?"

Amanda looked at the officer with the biggest look of annoyance she could muster, and James smiled mischievously, although he thought it was his innocent look. A look he used when he wanted to try to connive someone.

"Uh, nothing officer. Everything is fine," James quickly answered.

The police officer looked over at Amanda and slightly put his hand on his cuffs. "Is that true ma'am? Is everything okay?"

Amanda looked at James and then back at the officer before rolling her eyes at the both of them and storming out of the courthouse, not bothering to shield herself from the pouring rain that was falling.

2

*D*ylan! I'm not going to tell you twice. Get the toys cleaned up right now young man," Amanda called out to her son. Toys all over this house," she grumbled. Opening the refrigerator, she thought about her day at court. "One hundred dollars a month?! What a waste of my time." *The judge has no idea how he has screwed me over. How are we supposed to eat, to live with a hundred dollars a month?* Slamming the refrigerator shut, she turned towards the window and pulled the broken blind outwards in hopes that it would serve as cover for the entire window. She sighed when the loose bind gave way and fell to the floor. "Oh damn. Just my luck!" Putting her hand over her mouth to hold in her frustrated scream, she closed her eyes and breathed in deeply. It wasn't the broken blind that was the root of her anger but her life in total. No matter what she tried to do in life to make things better for her, she failed. Abandoned at the tender age of four by her mother and the absence of her father since conception, she was forced to learn to fend for herself. Yes, she had some points in her life where she felt was a win. Becoming the best stripper ever known in D.C; not daring to bring the heat and all her booty shaking and tongue magic to the stripper polls in Baltimore where someone may spot her and dime her out in front of her son was one of them. Making it on her own thus far was the greatest accomplishment. Even though it wasn't the best of circumstances, it sure beat living in a home with four girls to one bed and dealing with people the foster care system deemed appropriate and educated enough to run a group home. People who wanted a check and that was it; whatever happened to the girls in their care was none of their business once they were paid. Running away from the group home and proving that she could make it without anybody was huge for her. The little that she had was hers and she didn't have to share with anyone, except for her beloved son. Grabbing the half sheet that served as her kitchen tablecloth, she pulled open her junk drawer, picked up two nails, closed it and looked around. Spotting one of her boots in the living room, she walked over and grabbed it. *Hmm, not pointy enough.* Looking around once more, she saw one of her black skinny pointed heels and grabbed that, throwing the boot off to the side. Walking back into the kitchen, she hopped onto the sink, pulled her sheet up towards the window and used her shoe to bang the nails into the correct areas that would give her and her son adequate privacy. "There we go, that's better. I knew this shoe would come in handy one of these days."

10

"Mommy?"

Amanda turned towards her son's voice and smiled. "Yep?"

"I'm hungry. What's for dinner?"

"Hmmm… Let's see what we have. You know, I'm hungry too," she smiled.

"I hope it's not oatmeal again."

Thinking of the judge's judgment, she shook her head and used every fiber in her being to focus on her son and only him. Thoughts of James continued to burn its way into her brain, so she done what she taught herself to do; never show fear, disappointment, or negativity around Dylan.

Amanda smiled at her son, admiring him. "You are just too cute, son. Oatmeal is better than nothing at all, right?"

She was breaking inside and wished that she had more to offer but that was it. A tall box of oatmeal was what she relied on most to feed Dylan and herself. Except for the times when her depression and somberness stole her appetite and she chose not to eat at all.

"Yeah," Dylan sighed. "That's right Mom."

Pulling open the cabinet, she grabbed the oatmeal and the only two bowls she owned.

"Oh my goodness! He is too funny," Amanda laughed and clapped her hands in excitement as she watched her favorite comedian perform on the TV. Thankful for her neighbor who hooked her up with all the channels and not having to pay him a dime, well, she paid him, but it wasn't money, made her night. *It was boring as hell before he put the cable in. I am so glad he was finally able to make his way over here.* "I guess I need to try to get Dylan a TV with some of the child support money so he can get... who the hell am I fooling. I ain't got no extra money for an extra TV. Dylan is just going to have to chill in here to watch TV. That measly hundred dollars ain't going to get us far." Pulling the blanket over her body, she grabbed the newspaper that she was looking through earlier. Falling asleep the night before, she didn't finish looking through it. Laughing aloud again, she focused on the T.V and watched the host make a few corny jokes, which she found surprisingly funny, while waiting for the next comedian to make his or her way to the stage. "Oh no, not him. He's boring as hell." Pushing the mute button, she turned around on her left side and looked down at the newspaper. "I really need a job... fast." Skimming through the paper, she marked each section of interest carefully. "Uh-huh, this may be something," she mumbled as she circled the ad. Great benefits, no experience required. Oh... shoot... the job is only days and weekends," she muttered. "Who will babysit Dylan?"

"Mommy?"

Looking over to the door, she spotted her son staring at her with a frown on his face. "Yes baby? What's the matter?" Amanda sat up, put the paper down beside her, and motioned for her son to join her. "Did you have a bad dream?"

"No mommy. My heart hurts again."

Amanda sat up further. "Okay; everything is okay, son." Reciting her no fear, no disappointment, and no negativity mantra internally, she slid out of the bed.

"Lay down baby." Moving the blankets back, she helped her son hop into her bed. "I'm going to get your medicine, okay?"

"Okay Mommy."

Amanda smiled at her son, reassuring him. Although she smiled, she again, was dying inside. *I hate it when he is in pain. I hope it's not crisis pain*, she thought to herself as she went into the kitchen to grab her son's medicine.

3

*O*h, shut up. Just shut up, James! You are only doing this because you don't want to pay child support!" Amanda yelled.

"Wait a minute, hold on honey. We are not doing this for money purposes. We just feel it is better for Dylan if he comes to live with us," Evelyn Moore, her son's paternal grandmother, jumped in. "That's all."

"Ms. Moore, with all due respect, I can take care of my son. I don't need you or your child... your son to do it for me."

Amanda held back laughter at the look on Evelyn's face. In Amanda's mind, Ms. Moore was too bougie to fight and too uppity to curse someone out, so she felt free to pretty much say whatever she wanted. On the other hand, her son was the complete opposite, so Amanda stayed ready for whatever insult or ridiculous statements he threw her way.

"I see differently, Mandy."

"Right on time," Amada quipped.

"You don't even have food to feed him."

"I told you before to stop calling me that! My name is Amanda!"

"Okay, Amanda, please calm down. We only want what's best for my grandson."

Amanda looked away, focusing her eyes on the hand-painted artwork that lined the walls of the Moore family's dining room. She always secretly admired this home; careful not to make James and his family feel as if they had the "upper hand" over her. *They already feel that they are better than most people, why compliment them and make it easier for them to boast.* James' family home was well-kept and beautifully decorated, complements to the money that was left in a life insurance settlement that Evelyn's mother left for her a few years ago. *Me and Dylan need a house like this. Too bad I don't have someone around me that's going to leave us a thing. Not even a kiss my ass or go to hell...nothing at all.*

"We can make it temporary dear. Just until you get yourself together; maybe finish your classes. How does that sound?"

Amanda remained quiet and moved her eyes from the artwork to her keychains, grabbing the one that was shaped like a crab; the one that Dylan specially picked out on their complimentary Ocean City beach trip by one of her gracious and eager "*business associates*".

"We can even help with his medications," Evelyn continued.

16

Loosing focus on the artwork, she turned to Evelyn. "His medication?" Amanda sarcastically asked.

"Absolutely! We know he must have it for his sickle cell."

Damn, does this chick ever talk regular. Everything is yes dear or certainly dear. Like she's just full of riches. If it wasn't for her dead mama, she would be just as broke as me. Amanda cut her eyes towards James. *Oh, and his ass. I wish I could smack that smug smile off his face,* "So, you want to help with his *medication* now? Let me ask you both something."

"Anything dear," Evelyn smiled.

Amanda sighed and shook her head. *She got one more time to call me dear!* "Why do I have to deliver my child to you in order for you to help pay for his medicine? I mean, shouldn't you be doing that anyway?"

"I can answer that Ma."

"Yeah, you right. I should be doing that, and I will start as soon as he comes to live with us. I would do better than what you're doing and use his money that he gets monthly to pay for all the medication he needs. I wouldn't even ask the judge for child support."

Amanda looked sharply at James. "I cannot believe you James. What the hell is the matter with you?"

"Amanda, honey, listen. Like I said before, we just want what's best for Dylan."

17

"Yes, Ms. Moore, I heard you the first time! Well, I'm not giving you my son." Amanda got up and stormed towards the door. "Oh yeah, before I go, I have one last thing that I want to say."

"Why sure, go ahead honey," Evelyn gently responded.

"I know that you both only want to take Dylan so you can take his check. I'm not a fool. I'm not sure why because your mama left you with money for decades. I think ya'll just want to make my life hell and taking my son is the only way to do it. Well, you aren't getting my son and that's what the hell it is!" Amanda yelled.

"Oh okay, ight then. The bitch has spoken! We are not getting Dylan!"

"Bitch! I got yo' bitch!"

"Hey! That's enough!" Evelyn yelled at the top of her lungs before holding her chest and sitting down at the dining room table.

Evelyn reached under the table and pulled out an oxygen tank, startling Amanda. She stood by the door, confused. *Since when does that bitch need oxygen. I guess all her selfish shit she used to do is coming back on her.* Opening the door, she reluctantly stopped at the sound of James' voice.

"Hold up! Before you go…"

"Ma, looks like we need to move to plan two."

Amanda turned towards James. "Plan two? "What might that be?" she asked in an aggravated tone.

"Well, sweetie," Evelyn spoke through her shortness of breath as she continued to hold her chest. "We'll just see you in court."

Feeling dizzy, Amanda held onto the door for support. "Court?! "You will see *me* in court?" she yelled once she realized what was just said. *I hope the bitch dies slowly.* Amanda kept her eyes on Evelyn but showed no remorse. Her feeling was full hatred; not much room for any kind of sympathy. Putting her hands on her hips and pushing her jacket off to the side, she waited in shock for an answer that she was sure would be just as shocking.

"Why, yes dear. I will get my grandson and there is nothing that you can do about it."

"How? On what terms? I'm a good mother and no judge in their right mind would take my son away from me and give him to ya'll. Ya'll are too dysfunctional for that."

"A good mother? You tell me what judge would think that selling ass is a good role model for a six-year-old?"

"You son of a bi—"

"Oh no! I told you to stop it! Both of you!"

Amanda shook her head. "I can't believe you both are turning against me," she said as she looked at James and his mother as if they had lost their minds.

19

"James," she said in a forced, shrill voice, hoping that James or at least his mother would have some sympathy for her. "You know I have to do that from time to time just to make ends meet." Amanda forced tears, hoping that her new enemies would forget the entire conversation and let her go with the last bit of sanity she had left.

"Yes, we know, dear." Evelyn stood up, removed her oxygen mask, and pulled her wig down further on her head. "We know you must do that to make ends meet; to pay your rent. Let us help you, Amanda."

"You know what Ms. Moore? You and your sorry ass, good-for- nothing son, go and do what you feel you have to do." James smiled and put his arm around his mother. "Okay, you said it, so we will see you in court, Mandy."

"Yup, I guess you will. But remember one thing, I too have information about you and your poor excuse for a mother."

"Evelyn, that wig is still crooked as hell. Pull it to the left some. That raggedy ass stocking cap of yours is showing!" She yelled before opening the door and slamming it behind her.

irl, I don't know what I am going to do. Why do they want to cause me so much misery, Tracy? I've done nothing but be good to them," Amanda vented her issues to her best friend. The one friend who understood her and was able to feel the same pain she felt. Mainly because of the time they shared swapping hopes and dreams on a brighter future and better lives than what the group home had to offer.

"Girl, who knows. People like to see others die of misery. Misery loves company, you know. James is a low life who chooses to live with his mother because he has nothing going for himself and his mother welcomes him because she is lonely and miserable too. That's why they want to cause trouble for you."

Amanda chuckled, "Yes, I guess you're right. I am going to do everything in my power to keep those people from stealing my son."

"I feel you, girl. What do you plan to do?"

Amanda looked down, "I don't know yet."

"James and his mother, the witch, have their issues but they are not stupid. They know people and that can be hard for you when you go to court."

"Yep, I thought about that"

"Well, I am here for you if needed, you know that."

"Thanks, Tracy, I really appreciate all of your support."

"Sure, no problem, Mandy."

"Okay… bitch…you know I hate that name," Amanda said, laughing.

"Yeah, I know. Just burns you up, huh?"

"Yes! I do! so stop it!"

"And that's why I do it! Just to mess wit' you. Same reason why James do it so stop letting him know how much it pisses you off!"

"Yeah, you right. You are right girl. I gotta' stop letting that fool get the best of me."

"Yeah, you do. Do him like you used to that bitch…what was her name? Um…"

"Who…? April?"

"Yes! Her! Ignore him how you used to ignore her when she used to try to make us go to different rooms. You didn't give her no time. Do his ass the same way."

"Yeah, I hated her ass."

"Yes, and you hate his ass too so it should be easy for you."

Amanda giggled while fixing the back of her earring.

"Well, lady, I know you need to head out. Don't worry about Dylan, I got everything under control."

"Okay, thanks girl. Oh, and please don't forget he needs his medicine at—"

"Eight, I got it, Amanda. Just go already. Make me proud out there with those dudes."

"Ill, not at all. Just doing this because I have to. There is no rule that says I have to enjoy it."

"Shit, well, sex is sex. You may as well enjoy it and make money too."

"Girl bye! Once I pay this month's rent, I am done with this life." *Well, at least I hope so,* "Okay chick, thanks again for watching Dylan. I will be back as soon as I can."

Opening the door, Amanda walked out quickly while she still had the confidence needed to earn her rent money.

"What the hell is taking him so long? Ugh, I don't have all night," Amanda huffed as she stared out at the dimly lit parking lot of the Hardy Inn. Although she's been at the inn more times than she could count, she still felt nervous for being there. The motel was known for having men hanging around, only looking for one thing and one thing only… to be satisfied and to be satisfied quick with no interruptions and no claims. "Come on fool," Amanda huffed as she walked back to the bed and sat down. She glanced around at her surroundings, a habit she's been doing since she started her dealings at the motel and saw the same exact thing she always saw. The walls were dusty and was a dull yellow color, and the floor was carpeted with the ugliest brown carpet she's ever seen. Chuckling, she moved her feet around on the floor and looked over in the corner at the mold that was now a part of the actual wall. The room hasn't changed a bit and there was a chance that the owner, a former prostitute herself, wasn't going to change anything. Her pockets were her priority and nothing else, not even keeping up on building codes put into effect by the state of Maryland. Sighing, Amanda stood up and brushed her hands through her long orange weave and chuckled. "Here I am wearing this stupid ass wig and he ain't even here yet. I hate this damn thing and if it didn't put Willy in a *giving* mood, then it would definitely be in the trash where it belongs." Walking over to the partially shattered glass that was supposed to be a mirror, she studied her face as best she could through the cracks. "I should've put on gold lipstick this time." Out of all the guys she dealt with, Willy was the pickiest. He wanted her face, her hair, and her body to look exactly how he'd specified, or all bets were off. The only thing

24

he didn't care too much about were her lips; as long as she had some color on them, he was happy. Out of all five of her employers, Willy was her least favorite and she hated being with him, but he was one of the most established and was one of the highest paid lawyers in Baltimore. A well-respected defense attorney and black lives matter activists who represented his community to the fullest. The pay was incredible, and she needed every bit out of his pay that he was willing to give her. "Willy got that long money," she mumbled as she continued to comb through her wig. She loathed every Monday, Wednesday, and Friday simply because those were the days Willy wanted to meet her; to get his fix, as he called it. Ironically, those were the same days you would catch him on TV doing commentary for channel six, the station which featured the prostitution problems and where a lot of debating happened for victims of gun violence and other senseless acts. A true advocate indeed who, little did they know, was one of the men who enjoyed the work of a prostitute and had a pressing engagement with one right after the show was over. As soon as he turned his mic off, he was going to do the very thing that he and the other hosts were arguing about. "Damn, I can't stand laying in that nasty ass bed, waiting for an entire thirty minutes before we can go ahead and get it over with. Why can't he just take the damn pill early so he would be ready as soon as he got here." Moving her lips around in a small circle, she backed away from the mirror and looked over at the door. "I wonder why he wants to meet up with me so much instead of being at home with his wife. You would think she would be giving him some all the time. Even if it's just to keep him; to keep the money and the lifestyle in check." Chuckling, she shook her head and flopped down on the chair that sat next to the dresser. "I guess she wants something that she can actually feel. Even when the pills finally start working, his shit is still as small as the led on a pencil." Laughing, she looked over at the door and abruptly stopped as it opened. "Finally," she huffed before quickly combing through her wig again and standing up as she mentally prepared to have Willy's seventy-two-year-old hands all over her twenty-four-year-old body while they both anxiously waited for the pills to take effect.

5

"O kay baby, you can have the ice cream, but be very careful not to spill it on your new shirt," Amanda said as she smiled at her son.

"Okay mommy, no problem."

"No problem? Where did you learn to say, no problem?" Amanda laughed.

"Auntie Tracy says it. She always says, okay baby, no problem."

Amanda laughed and playfully nudged her son. "Well, at least that's all she says... around you anyway."

"Okay little man, you have twenty minutes to get your play on and then we have to leave."

Amanda sat down on the closest bench to the play area and watched as her son climb onto the monkey bars. *Thank goodness for the extra ends from last night*, she thought to herself as she watched Dylan play. *The rent is paid, and I even had enough to buy that cute outfit and put food in the house. A few more times with Willy and we will be on easy street.* Picking with her nails and looking at the kids play, she tried to clear her mind of any and everything. Instead of a mind full of polluted thoughts about the pressures of her life, she worked to fill it with fantasies of a new home and the scent of a new car. Along with all the money that would seep over to amounts that she couldn't count by hand. Long money; the kind of money that caused people to sit up straight and address her as such. The kind of money that when she walked into a bank, the teller shows her to a whole different area of the bank; reserved for the rich folk.

"Cute kid; I like his shirt."

Amanda looked over at the sound of the voice, shielding her eyes with her hands from the blinding sunlight. Liking the tall, muscle bound frame she saw, she substituted a wave with the nod of her head. "Thanks. I'm sure he's going to mess it up," she said in her "he can get voice".

"I'm Dorian."

Amanda reached over to shake Dorian's extended hand. "Nice to meet you Dorian. My name is Amanda."

"Amanda, that's a pretty name."

"Thanks," she said as she tried to contain her blushing smile.

"So, how old is he?"

"He's six, going on sixty, Amanda chuckled.

"Oh yeah, he's at the golden age," Dorian laughed.

"Yes, tell me about it. Kids are such a mess at six. *That-a-boy sir, talk to me about my kid to work your way right on in. I see you.*

"Yes, they are, but enjoy it. They grow up so fast. My daughter is twelve."

"Uh, yes, pre-teen stage. The rough years."

"Dylan, you're going too fast, slow down!"

Amanda and Dorian paused their conversation and focused on Dylan.

"Active little guy huh?"

"Huh…active is an understatement. He's all over the place," she laughed.

"Yeah, boys usually are."

There was another pause before either of them said a word. Amanda wasn't sure on what to say next. The men she's been having conversation with lately were men that only spoke of one thing and components related to it. All other cordial conversation was at a minimum with those guys.

"So, Ms. Amanda, are you from around this way? I've never seen you here before."

Yes…that works…small talk questions. "No, we are from the other side of town. I like to take my son to nice parks whenever I can and this time it happens to be at this one," she smiled.

29

"Well, I'm glad you decided to come to this side of town."

"You know what?"

"No, what?"

"I have never seen anybody as beautiful as you. If I asked you out to dinner, would you go?"

Amanda smiled nervously before answering. "Well, you haven't asked so I guess you wouldn't know until you do." *Good come back…so, all isn't lost.*

"Okay, the pressure is on," Dorian chuckled. "Okay, now I'm asking. Will you go out to dinner with me?"

Amanda looked out at her son, careful not to jump to quickly. *Always make them wait a minute*, she heard Tracy's voice.

"Hmmm… well…"

"Well…?"

"Maybe."

"Why should I go out to dinner with you? I mean, I could have a boyfriend. You never asked me if I had one."

"Yes, and I could have a girlfriend, but what's your point? I didn't ask you to marry me; I just asked if you would like to go somewhere and grab a bite."

Amanda glared at her new companion. "Well, nicely put but when a man asks a lady out to dinner, it usually means much more than the food." Growing prouder of herself by the minute, she sat back and waited for Dorian to answer. *I still know how to be out here in these streets; I still got my flirt game. He has a cute smile and the whitest teeth I've ever seen.*

"Okay. Ight. So, you are the "go-deeper" kind of girl.

"Yep, that I am," she chuckled.

Looking out at Dylan, she stood to get a clearer view of the little boy he was talking to. She watched as they laughed at something and ran off together to the swings.

Sitting back down and turning her attention back to Dorian, she politely smiled. "So, Dorian, do you have a girlfriend?"

"A girlfriend. That is important to you, huh?"

Amanda shrugged her shoulders. "Yeah, it is. I've learned to ask questions up front so there will be no surprises later. No need to start a friendship if you have a girlfriend. Woman tend not to like their men having friendships with other women these days."

"Oh…kay; it sounds like you've been in that type of situation before."

"Yep, well, something like that," she nodded her head. "Years ago."

"So, Ms. Lady, do you agree to go out to dinner with me? We can talk about your past friendships; let you get it all out in the open."

Amanda laughed aloud. "You never answered my question."

"Hmmm, the question of having a girlfriend. Okay, Ms. Amanda. To answer your question, no, I do not have a girlfriend."

"Well, that's good to know," she smiled.

"Now that I've answered the number one question, it is time for you to answer mine. Will you please go out to dinner with me?"

"Dylan, I am not going to keep repeating myself young man!" she called out, careful not to seem too anxious.

Amanda kept her eyes on Dylan while Dorian kept his eyes on her.

"I tell you what, Ms. Amanda. What if we start by exchanging phone numbers? Would that work for you?"

Aw damn, I should've known he was going to ask for my number. I can't tell this man that I can't afford a phone "No, not necessary," she quickly answered. "I would love to go out to dinner with you. Just name the place and I will meet you there." Amanda began to feel hot from embarrassment; doing everything in her power not to let it show.

"I prefer to remain a gentleman and pick you up."

"Oh no, it's all good. I will meet you. Just name the place, day, and time and I will be there."

There was an uncomfortable pause before the conversation continued.

"Ight, what type of food do you like?"

32

"Well, burgers and fries are okay with me," Amanda answered.

"Wow, burgers and fries, huh?"

"What? What's wrong with that?" she giggled.

"Nothing, nothing at all. But I was thinking more along the lines of sushi or steak."

"Sushi...? Raw fish...? No, thank you," Amanda said, laughing, thankful that her jitteriness and embarrassment by not having a phone didn't show and ruin the mood.

"Hey, don't knock it until you try it," Dorian laughed. "I tell you what, let's meet tomorrow night. Say around six? I know this place that has the best sushi rolls money can buy. What do you say?"

"Um, okay. Where is this place?" she reluctantly asked.

"Dominick's."

"Dominick's," Amanda repeated. "I've never heard of it."

"It's right on the corner of Sunset and Main Street. You will love it, I promise."

"Okay… I guess. I will see you there then. I'm not making any promises of trying the raw fish, though."

Amanda and Dorian both laughed aloud before shaking hands to seal the date.

6

$\mathcal{H}$ere we go, Amanda mumbled as she looked around at the one place she hated more than anything else in the world. Well, besides the foster home she lived in as a child, the courthouse. Her stomach burned with knots, her head was on fire from the headache that she'd had since she opened her eyes and dragged herself out of bed, and her fingers and toes were numb. Looking over at the other side of the courtroom, she frowned at the sight of James and his mother. *Bitches… sitting there laughing and talking like they have no problems. Who works so hard to take a child away from his mother? Who does that? Shit, I know girls who don't pay their kids any mind at all and nobody tries to take them away. If anything, they get mad child support and food stamps. Why the hell am I so different? Why are they trying to take my child? Well, whatever, they are not getting my son. I'm a good mother. No judge will take my child away from me.* Turning her head and closing her eyes, she replayed the events of the day in her head, still in shock at how James did a complete three-sixty on her and turned the courtroom into the movie Losing Isiah. He was Samuel L. Jackson all of a sudden and she was Jessica Lang, trying to fight against the fact that she is her son's mother and she deserves to have the right to be with him. The longest and hardest day she's ever had in court. *Every time I come here, I get a smack in the face. When I was younger, I was sent to that damn home. When I was a teenager and had to check a bitch, I was sent to anger management class for six months; which was a complete waste of my time, and I only get a couple of dollars of child support. Maybe today will be different. Yeah, today, the court will actually do the right thing this time and not take my child away from me.* Sighing, she twisted in her seat and looked back at Tracy. Tracy gave a reassuring smile, causing her to relax a bit. Her fingers and toes were still numb, but her headache was easing off and the rumbling in her stomach shifted to light butterflies.

"How long does it take for a judge to make a decision?"

"It shouldn't be too much longer. Hopefully, she'll be back soon," Tracy whispered.

Turning back around, Amanda put her hands in her head and inhaled.

The judge's door opened causing Amanda to lift her head quickly. Standing up, she quickly looked back at Tracy and glanced over at James and his mother before fixing her eyes on the judge.

"Have a seat."

Amanda found the judge's soft-spoken voice relaxing and hoped that she would be different than all the rest of the judges and do what's right for her for a change.

"I've gone over all the paperwork that was submitted and I've thought long and hard about my decision."

Amanda felt nauseas and a deep burring within the pit of her stomach. *My last chance…*

"Your Honor, may I please say something?" she blurted out; feeling as if she needed to say more to convince the judge to rule in her favor.

The judge cut her eyes over at Amanda before she answered. "Sure, Ms. Ingram. What would you like to say?"

Trying to think of something to say to convince the judge, she closed her eyes and quickly opened them back up. "I-I don't have a lot of money, that's true." She paused, looked over at James, blinked hard and looked back at the judge. "But I love my son. My son is very sick, and he needs to be with me. Please don't grant those people custody. I'm begging you."
Amanda studied the judge's face but saw no emotion. Suddenly, the warm voice didn't match the face and it bugged her.

"Ms. Ingram, I understand your point, but my job is to do what's best for the child."

The courtroom was so silent that you could hear the tiniest pin drop. Amanda stood still, holding her breath so tight that she thought she would pass out at any minute.

"Temporary custody granted to Mr. Moore. Case dismissed."

"No!" Amanda cried. "Please, Your Honor." Amanda pleaded with the judge until she was out of earshot.

Gleefulness jolted from James' side of the courtroom while Amada's side was quiet. Her heart raced and her breath was short as dizziness consumed her, causing her to sit down.

"It's going to be okay, Amanda," Tracy soothed as she stood up from her seat and tenderly touched Amanda's shoulder.

Tears began to burn in the corners of her eyes as she sat still, wondering what she has done so wrong to have God turn against her. *What did I do? God, what did I do to have my child taken from me? I only try to do what's best for my baby, and you allow them to take him. Why?*

"Amanda come on, let's go. It's all going to be okay."

"No, it's not Tracy. That lady took my son away!"

"Amanda, calm down. You are in the court room. Don't let those people get the best of you, girl. Pull yourself together."

Amanda wiped the tears away from her eyes, taking Tracy's advice. Slowly standing, her legs felt wobbly and her headache was back at full force. "I got to get out of here."

Finding her balance, she slowly turned towards Tracy and hugged her. More tears fell from her eyes as her best friend embraced her and whispered encouraging words. Finally feeling as if she could walk, she walked out of the courtroom and into the cold hallway. Amanda felt like someone had taken the air out of lungs.

"I can't believe this is happening, Tracy. Like for real, how can the judge do this to me?"

"I know, but it's going to be okay. Just watch and see."

"Yeah, it's going to be okay, Mandy."

A cold shudder worked its way down Amanda's spine before she quickly whipped towards James. "I hate your ass! You will regret this, I promise you."

"Oh, is that right? Is that a threat, Amanda?"

Amanda balled her fist to match the incredible urge to sucker punch James and knock him down. She wanted to deliver pain to him to match the pain she was feeling.

"You know, I can go back into the court room and ask to speak with the judge. Tell her that you are now communicating threats. I can easily go in and tell her that you're ready to throw those hands. Oh yeah and to thank her again for giving me my son. How does that sound?"

Amanda opened her mouth to speak but her brain wouldn't do its part and form any words.

"Hell, you should be thanking me! You know you got a nigga or what do ya'll call them? A john… yeah that's what ya'll hoes say… johns or is it tricks now? You got one waiting for you tonight. It will be easier for you to get out and do what you do since Jordan is finally where he belongs."

Amanda stared at James, not believing that she allowed herself to love him at one point in her life.

"Come on Amanda. Don't let that low life get to you," Tracy slowly encouraged while gently pulling Amanda's arm. "Come on girl."

Feeling defeated and drained, Amanda looked at Tracy with tears in her eyes before walking away.

Laying on the floor in her room, Amanda felt like a zombie. A week had passed since Dylan was removed from her home and given to James and his mother. She still couldn't believe how she was treated at court and afterwards. "Five police… they sent five police to my house to get my son. Like I'm some rapist or something. Or like I got guns and shit up in here, ready to blast their asses." Sitting up, she wiped her eyes and threw the tissue into the pile she created. The tears wouldn't stop no matter what she did or how hard she tried to think of something else. All she had on her mind was her son… and revenge. The day in court resurfaced in her mind and she smacked her lips before more tears expelled. Where the hell did he get all that from anyway?! I don't understand how… the hard knock on the door stopped Amanda's rant.

"Amanda! Open up! It's me!"

Sighing, Amanda sat on the floor a few seconds longer before getting up and walking to the door. She wiped more tears away with her left hand and turned the knob with her right, letting Tracy in.

"Hey girl!"

Giving a quick wave, Amanda kept her mouth closed as she walked back to her bedroom.

"Alright now, get yourself out of that nasty ass funk! It's all going to work out."

Flopping down on her bed, she glanced at Tracy and put her head down. "Easy for you to say. You didn't have a judge tell you that you are a bad mother, rip your child away and close the book on *you*."

"Yes, the hell I did. Dylan is my godson, so the judge took him away from me too."

"Yeah," Amanda muttered but kept her head down.

"Bitch… get up!"

Amanda sighed and continued to sit still.

"I said get your ass up!"

"Tracy, leave me alone. I don't feel like—"

"I don't care! You are sitting up in here, allowing some bitches to make you weak. You goin' just let them do you like that? Where is your fight? Where is the bitch I know from west Baltimore that will knock another bitch out with one punch?! Huh?! Get up Amanda!"

"I can't! I don't have anymore fight left in me. Amanda stood up and clutched her chest. I'm tired of fighting Tracy. I've been fighting since I was four years old! I'm tired."

Tracy walked close to Amanda and forcefully grabbed her by the shoulders. "Then this is the time for you to dig as hard as you can. Pull Amanda! Just like that chick Yolanda says; you know the girl on the Her Intuition Movement Podcast. You have to rely on your own strength. It's there, you just have to pull on it. I just listened to her this morning and she was talking about it."

Amanda pushed Tracy away and allowed a fresh set of tears to flow from her eyes and onto her face. "Dylan," she whispered softly.

"Yes, Dylan. He's your reason for finding your fight. You still got it girl. It's just that your pain is blinding you."

Amanda walked into the kitchen and grabbed her keychain. She gently rubbed the crab shaped one and stared off into the distance. "Yes, for Dylan," she recited as a renewed strength and power began to burn from deep within.

7

*L*ook, I came here for one reason and one reason only. I am not interested in anything else, okay?" Amanda stared at the gentleman behind the counter with fury in her eyes.

"Um, okay, ma'am. I apologize. I was only offering because we have some great deals here and I thought you might be interested, that's all."

"Apology accepted," Amanda sighed. "Now back to the reason that I am here."

"Yes, ma'am, but I need to see some I.D. Do you have any on you? Once I see your I.D, then I will be able to get you what you need."

Amanda threw her expired license down on the counter. "Do you need anything else?" She asked with irritation. "I don't have all day, you know."

"Yes, I understand ma'am, but I have to follow protocol. Those things aren't toys, *you know*."

Amanda frowned at the chubby guy standing behind the counter. *I know he ain't getting slick with me.*

"Just hurry, please!" she blurted, a bit too loudly.

The salesman shook his head before he walked over to the large glass counter and pulled out the shiny object.

"Do you know how to use this?"

Amanda stared at the salesman with a blank stare, showing no emotion.

"Uh okay, I can't force you to answer my questions, so here you go."

Amanda snatched the object and her expired license out of the salesman's hand and stormed out the door, not bothering to look back.

Letting out a shrill gasp, Amanda quickly opened her eyes to darkness. Her throat burned like fresh hot coals and her chest felt as if knives were being poked repeatedly through her skin. Her muscles were sore, and her head was on fire. Mustering up as much strength as she could, she moved her left arm only to find that it was stuck in between her thigh and the side of what felt like a hardened cushion. "What is...?" She started but the sting from her throat was too much. Deciding to ignore the aches and pains, she cleared her throat and tried again. Still, the burn was too much. *Pull on your strength from within*, she heard her favorite Inspirational speaker, Yolanda, whisper. Closing her eyes and inhaling deeply, she cleared her throat once more, finally removing the clutter that was glued tightly inside her. Taking full advantage of her cleared throat, she yelled out. "Some…," stopping, she winced from the pain that burned, this time, from her chest. Lightly coughing, she tried again. "Somebody! Please, I can't breathe!" Short of breath, she closed her eyes and waited impatiently for her oxygen levels to rebuild. Inhaling deeply, she went for it. "Somebody, please help me!" She screamed as loud as she could from the cold, clammy box that she was stuffed into.

"Yeah, I got her in here, man. Let's hurry up before she finds a way to get out."

Gasping, she held her breath just long enough to pay attention to the voices. *James…*? She listened closely as men talked from outside, wondering if her mind was playing tricks on her. The geto boys' song, mind playing tricks on me, popped into her head and she chuckled. *Maybe I'm crazy as hell. I—*

"Come on man, damn!"

James? She mouthed quickly. *That is James… that sorry bastard.* She coughed and prepared her body before she let out another call for help. "Help me!" she yelled. This time, her voice was strong and full of fire! "James!" An enormous wave of nausea took control of her stomach and her throat and chest

47

began to burn again. Ignoring the agony, she continued her fight. "Let me out of here right now!" she managed to holler before becoming lightheaded and winded. To her surprise, the box quickly flew open. Amanda sucked up as much air as she possibly could before working to get out of the homemade coffin. Slapping her arms as hard as she could onto the edge of the box, her fingers slipped from the light rain fall that was falling. "James?! What the hell?!" Although she couldn't see him, she knew he was there; she could feel him.

"James!"

Tears began to burn within the corner of her right eye and her fingers began to feel numb. *Pull from within*, she whispered before grabbing onto the side of the coffin, this time, ignoring the dampness. She pulled herself up onto the side and sighed loudly. An incredible heaviness weighed her down as she continued to wiggle her upper body.

"James! Damn it," she cried out in a voice that she didn't recognize. "Ugh," she yelled loudly until she lifted her upper body and maneuvered it out of the box. In pain, yet determined, she used everything in her to pull herself completely out of the coffin. "Ow!" She winced in pain as her body hit the ground. *Ouch.* Opening her eyes wide, she allowed the tears that were stinging in the corners to fall freely. She surveyed her surroundings through her clouded eyes only to see nothing but bare trees staring back at her.

48

"James…"

"What?"

Amanda looked up in the eyes of the devil himself, starring down at her like he was waiting on her to sell her soul. In an instant, the heavy weight that she's felt since she's been in this predicament was completely lifted off of her and she jumped up. Finally to her feet, she charged at James but landed on the ground instead. Quickly turning over, she was met eye to eye with a 9-millimeter pistol staring back at her. In a matter of seconds, Amanda's rage quickly turned to dread and fear. "James, please," she quickly begged. "Think of our son," she pleaded with tears falling down her face.

"Oh, so now you want to beg," James taunted.

Amanda continued to stare at the gun that was pointed directly at her head.

"You had lots of time to make this right, Mandy. You chose this, not me."

Amanda closed her eyes as James pulled the trigger. Surprised that she was still alive, Amanda quickly opened her eyes to see that she was in her home and her bed. Breathing deeply, she pulled herself out of bed, giving her entire body a once over to make sure everything was still intact. Taking a long, deep breath, she looked over at the television as an infomercial displayed on the screen. Taking long deep breaths, she took full advantage of her lungs and all the power that came with them. "Damn," she whispered as she wiped the beads of sweat that were forming on the top of her forehead. Putting her feet on the floor, she sat on the edge of her bed. As wild as her dream was, it was beginning to blur from her mind as Dylan eased his way in. *I got to get my child back. Why would a judge... a woman... take a child away from another woman? What kind of shit is that?* Amanda felt her muscles tense as thoughts of the judge and the case itself joined her son within the depths of her mind. Getting up, she walked quickly to the window and looked out of the broken blinds. *Where did they get all those pictures from? How does James even know where I be and who I deal with?* Looking at nothing but the stars in the night's sky, she began to think of her action plan. *I bet his mama paid somebody to watch me... Bitch... I hate her ass.* "No need to continue to think about this, it's time to act," she said aloud as she walked back to her bed and sat down. "I know I'm not going to get any sleep now," she said to herself as she grabbed the remote and flipped through the stations, in search of a late-night comedy special.

8

"Have you lost your mind, Amanda? You can't go in there like that," Tracy angrily whispered.

"Shhh, hush girl," Amanda hissed. "I didn't say I was going to do it; I just simply said that was an option."

"Well, that shouldn't even be an option either, Amanda. "Think about it, your son can get hurt. You can't run up on nobody like that and think they ain't going to react. You don't know what them people got going on over there."

"Right, and that's exactly why I need to get my son away from them. James don't give a damn about Dylan; just long enough to get his hands on Dylan's check."

"That's the thing I don't get. I mean, why would James need or want Dylan's money when his mama got all that money from his grandmother?"

Amanda looked at Tracy and shook her head. *Why does it even matter? All these fuckin' questions.* "Because his mama doesn't share her money. James is basically on his own with

51

extra shit. His mama lets him stay with her, but she don't give him money to get his shit."

"Shit? What shit?"

Amanda chuckled. "His pills."

"Oh bitch, I thought you was getting ready to tell something new. I thought he was taking his mama's pills," Tracy laughed, stood up and stretched.

"Girl bye! You know that heffa ain't sharing her shit with nobody. Not even her precious son of bitch son of hers."

"I don't like it. I think you should fight them like they are fighting you. Get a lawyer and—"

"A lawyer. Really? Where the hell am I going to get some money to get a lawyer? Aren't you the one who said she was looking for the bitch from west Baltimore? Well, here I am."

"Uh, legal aid has lots of lawyers that can help you and yeah, the bitch in you, but not on them… on yourself! Pick the bitch up in you to pull yourself together. Not to do that crazy mess you talkin' bout."

Amanda sat quietly, mentally making the decision to remain quiet about her plans going forward.

"So, what do you want to eat today? I was thinking steak."

Amanda looked up at her friend with a disapproving look on her face. "Girl, you know I don't have any money for—"

"Steak; I know, girl. It's on me. You know I got you."

"Nah, I'm not really hungry Tracy but thanks anyway."

"Aw, come on, Amanda. You really should stop starving yourself, girl. You need to eat."

Amanda looked at her friend with a slight frown on her face. "I'm not starving myself, Tracy. I just don't have an appetite. I mean, how can I sit and eat steak when I don't know if my son has eaten today? How can I sit here and act like everything is all good and I don't know if those people know how to give my son his medicine?" Amanda waited a few seconds before continuing. "My son has sickle cell Tracy and he has to be cared for the right way." Amanda felt a wave of tears forming in the corners of her eyes. "I mean what if he has a crisis and needs to go to the hospital?"

Wiping the tears away quickly, Amanda looked away from her friend, embarrassed that she allowed herself to go into another fit.

"Oh, Amanda, it's okay, girl. I hear you and you have every right to be concerned, but Dylan will be just fine. James and the bitch might be crazy as hell, but they aren't going to let anything happen to your son. Dylan is a part of their family; they wouldn't hurt him."

Amanda slowly released her tightened muscles as she listened to her friend's attempt to pacify her concerns. "Yeah, I know, but Dylan has to have his medicine every day. You know how irresponsible James can be; he might forget to give it to him. Especially if he's high." Looking to her friend for more comfort, Amanda fixed her eyes on Tracy.

"I don't care how high he gets, he ain't stupid enough to let something happen to Dylan. Your baby daddy ain't shit but I can promise you that he won't let anything happen."

Amanda looked down at the kitchen table, working hard to relax her mind. "Yeah, I guess… I need to chill."

"Yes, you do, and I have just the thing," Tracy said while walking towards the mini wine rack that sat on her kitchen counter.

Amanda looked up at Tracy and smiled. "I will grab the glasses," she said, thankful that she was beginning to feel better about her messy situation. *It feels awkward not having to worry about Dylan. Awkward but at the same time, kinda good to get a break.* The minute her thoughts surfaced to the forefront of her brain, the guilt began to take over. *Oh damn… What kind of mother am I to say this is a break when my child has been ripped away from me?*

"Yep," Tracy cheerfully said as she proceeded to grab the wine.

Stopping at the counter, Amanda rubbed her head and looked back at Tracy. *And how can she be all smiles and shit when my son has been taken?* Sighing, she reluctantly grabbed the wine glasses and sat them on the table.

"Yep, this is exactly what you need. Get some of this wine up in you."

Amanda sat down at the kitchen table and put her head down.

"Come on, sit up, and drink."

Lifting her head slowly, Amanda watched Tracy pour the red wine into her glass. Taking a small sip, she forcefully relaxed her shoulders and waited for the wine to kick in.

"Okay," Tracy said as she poured the wine into her glass and sat down in the chair across from Amanda. "I have some cold cuts in the fridge. How about sandwiches and chips?"

"Nope, not hun—"

"Hungry, I know but you still need to eat something."

Amanda sighed and kicked off her shoes to relax further. Glancing up at the clock, her eyes grew wide. *Eight o'clock... did they give Dylan his meds?* She looked on the table at Tracy's phone and grabbed at it. "Maybe I should call over there. I should call and... Damn it!"

"What?! Girl you scared the shit out of me! What you are yelling about?"

"That bastard changed his number so I can't call and it's eight o'clock. I should go over there."

"No, you're going to stay right here and get drunk with me. Dylan is fine girl."

Saying a quick, silent prayer for her son, she moved the agonizing thoughts to the back of her mind, intentionally bringing the thought of her new friend Dorian to the forefront. Taking another sip, longer than the first one, she anxiously waited for the effects of the wine to take over and to carry her to bliss. Yeah it was the cheap wine, but it was better than nothing. Sitting still, she thought of Dorian and how different he'd seemed than all the other guys she's met. Something about him lured her to him; wanting to get to know him better on a whole different level type feeling. Beginning to feel tingly, she smiled.

"Oh girl, I forgot to tell you about my new friend."

"I'm assuming it's a dude by that smile on your face or is it the wine?"

"The wine," Amanda chuckled goofily.

"Yeah right. Only some potential pen can get you all giddy. Well, the good pen not that you get when you trying to pay a bill."

"Bitch…"

Amanda laughed with Tracy as the two continued to sit at the table, both drinking their problems away.

"Girl, he is fine. It's been a minute since I actually wanted to get to know somebody."

"See… pen"

Amanda shook her head and drank more of her drink. "More than just sex. I wanna get to know him. Like move in type getting to know him."

"Girl bye wit' all that. You just met him. You got to give him some time to fuck up before you make that call. You know these dudes be all good in the beginning and change up on you when they get in. Like yo' baby daddy. Member him?"

"My baby daddy was just some baller at the club that was throwing money at me and only me, paid me mad bread to give him some and I accidently got pregnant. Now stuck with his ass all for a quick five minutes of feeling nothing. A big ass waste of my time."

Tracy laughed and Amanda chuckled.

"Girl I don't see what those girls be seeing in him. He ain't slanging nothing."

"I knew his ass was overcompensating for something."

Feeling good, Amanda fully relaxed and allowed the wine to take control of her body and her mind.

9

*S*crubbing the scent of old spice and a strong musk off her body, Amanda allowed the heat of the hot water to comfort her and to help remove the thoughts of her deeds a few hours earlier. "I hate the way that man smells," she said aloud as she continued to wash. Dabbing more of the silk-feeling and rose-smelling body wash onto her body, she inhaled deeply. "Yes, that's better," she whispered as she continued her quest to remove the stench of her loathsome lover off her. He was nasty and repulsive, yes, but he was her number one. The one who paid the highest bills for her and would sometimes give her extra. All the others weren't as generous, so she made sure to treat him particularly well. "At least the electric bill will be paid before those fools come out here to turn it off," she said as she focused her attention on her face; working overtime to remove the wet kisses that her employer for the evening planted on her. "If only he didn't want to *make love*; kissing and shit. Damn," she mumbled as she scrubbed her face hard with the extra washcloth she brought into the bathroom with her. "Well, it is what it is," she whispered as she thought of the events that took place a few hours earlier. Feeling cleaner; as clean as she was going to feel after one of her jobs, she used her right foot to turn the shower off and pushed the shower curtain off to the side. Heading out of the shower, she dried off quickly, draped her towel around her and headed out of the bathroom and into the cool hallway. Walking into her bedroom, she flipped on the television and sat down on her bed. Looking around her nearly empty bedroom, she sighed. "I got to do better," she mumbled. "It's my job to give Dylan a better life than the one I had." Laying across her bed and allowing her nakedness to become one with the air from the ajar window that filled her bedroom, she smiled and thought of her baby boy. Although she missed him and wanted him home with her, she couldn't help but to feel a sense of freedom. She loved her son with all her heart, but he was a lot to handle. His illness alone took up the majority of her time and his tender age gave her a run for her money. Her eyes wandered to the pictures on the wall across form her bed and she smiled. "Dylan, mommy will get you back home again, I promise. I will do whatever it takes." The familiar sting began to burn her eyes and she quickly dismissed it. "Uh-uh… I am done with all the crying and feeling sorry for myself; it's time to act," she said aloud as she pulled her covers down and grabbed both pillows for comfort, getting under her covers, she sighed as she forgot to turn the lights off. *Fuck it, they can stay on for the night*. "Shit," she chuckled. "I got to be crazy if I think I'ma keep those lights on all night. I can barely pay the damn bill as it is." Getting up quickly, she ran to the other side of her room, flipped the light switch off and, hurriedly got back into her cool bed. A strong wind blew through her room from the window. "Ohhh," she muttered and pulled the covers over her before grabbing the remote and flipping through the channels. "Maybe I can find a good comedy special on tonight," she smiled. Looking down at the remote, a gift that she'd acquired for her nightly services, she frowned. It was confusing to see so many extra buttons. It was nothing like the small, basic black remote that she was accustomed to all her life. Giving a little sex brought so many gifts to her home that she was finally beginning to feel like she could compete with the rest of the world. "I need to figure out how to use this thing," she mumbled while fingering the buttons. Eyeing the tools section on the remote, she pushed each key to see its function. "Thanks to Charles, I have such a *fancy* addition to my TV," she chuckled. "Those men will buy anything just to get a piece of ass," she said aloud as she continued to fumble with her gift. "Ah ha!" she exclaimed as a bunch of titles popped onto the screen. Another gust of air filled her space and she shuttered. Too tired to get up again to close the window, she ignored the cool breeze and kept her attention on her gift. Flipping through the list, she found a list of comedy titles and selected the first

61

one. "Finally figured it out," she smiled with an accomplished grin. A restaurant commercial began, reminding her of the dinner date with Dorian that she agreed to a few days ago. She smiled and closed her eyes as his face worked its way into her mind and his voice invisibly soothed her ears. She began to relax, allowing the thoughts of Dorian to whisk her away into her own private island; with no one around but him, her, and Dylan. Amanda opened her eyes to see a popcorn commercial floating across the screen. "Oh damn. Why did they have to throw that up here? I hate to get up, but I want some," she said aloud as she threw the covers off her body, rushed to close the window and head off into the kitchen. Grabbing the microwaveable popcorn from her bare cabinet, she popped the bag into another one of her exchanges, her microwave, and relaxed her elbows onto the cabinet, waiting patiently as her popcorn began to pop. She looked around at the old cabinets and the rusted refrigerator and frowned. *I need a change.* "Out of all the people in the world, why do I have it so bad? I hate this place." *When all else fails, begin to pray*, she heard Tracy's voice. Closing her eyes, she opened her mouth, but nothing came out. She wasn't sure on how to pray since it's been a while since she's spoken a word to God. "God, I need you," she started. Feeling a bit weird, a bit like a hypocrite, she wasn't sure if she should continue. *I don't think God listens to girls who sell their bodies.* Looking at basically nothing, she rubbed both of her arms. *Or does he?* Not sure if He does or doesn't, she continued... just in case. "I need your help," she looked up and cried out. "I can't do this by myself and I am tired of living this way, Lord." Taking a deep cleansing breath, she allowed her mind freedom. "I know that God is listening," she said to herself as she waited for the last minute to finish on the microwave. *One day, I am going to have more than enough money to get me and my baby out of here, I just have to find a way to do it.* The microwave beeped and Amanda quickly opened it. Removing the bag, she tore it open and walked back into her bedroom. Flopping down on the bed and throwing a few buttered pieces into her mouth, she grabbed her pillows and returned to her comfy state that she was in moments before.

My life changed for the better with just a simple phone call and yours can too. Pick up the phone and dial now! Stop putting your future on hold; begin an exciting career now. Financial Aid available for those who qualify.

Amanda sat up and focused her attentiveness on the television. A list of careers flowed on the screen, further grabbing Amanda's attention.

I got a free computer when I signed up and financial Aid paid all my expenses. I now have the career I always wanted. Don't let your future go to waste. Call the number on your screen today.

Amanda grabbed her son's coloring book and a crayon that he had left on the box that served as her nightstand and quickly jotted the number down before the commercial went off the screen. "Hmm, I think I will call this number," she said quietly. "I need a change," she continued as she placed the coloring book back onto its rightful place. *Maybe God did hear me.* Popping more popcorn into her mouth, she smiled, feeling a sense of pride for the first time in years. "I haven't felt like this since Dylan was born." A sense of relief filled her mind as she focused her eyes onto the television, readying herself for a night filled with laughter.

"I'll try anything once," Amanda said slowly to her dinner date as she watched him dip his sushi roll into a thick creamy sauce.

"You have to acquire a taste and once you do that, I promise you, you will be eating it all the time. Dominick's has the best sushi in all of Baltimore and this place doesn't disappoint," he assured her.

Amanda smiled at Dorian, allowing herself to have a good time. "Okay, I will try a small piece," she reluctantly said as she grabbed one of the small rolls on Dorian's plate. Taking a small bite, she chewed slowly, working overtime to clear her mind of any negative thoughts about eating fish that nobody took the time to cook. *I can't believe I am eating raw fish*, she thought quietly as she continued to chew. "It's not bad," she smiled at Dorian and popped the remaining piece into her mouth.

"Yes! See? I told you," Dorian said with a big bright smile.

Amanda studied Dorian as she continued to chew.

Damn, look at those dimples. This man is so fine. Her mind began to wander to places that it shouldn't go on the first date. Thoughts of wild, butt naked sex took control and she blushed. She quickly stopped her mind from going haywire as thoughts of her naked body lay on top of Dorian while his manhood rummaged through her wet pit of ecstasy. Instead, she fixed her mind to think of nothing but the exact moment in which she was living.

"So, Ms. Amanda, tell me more about yourself," Dorian asked, helping Amanda to reach her goal of a free mind.

Well, I certainly can't tell this man about my life! He would run wild, right out the front door and leave me here to pay for a meal that I can't afford. "What would you like to know?" she asked, playing it cool, adding a sparkling smile.

Amanda watched Dorian as he took a small sip of his wine.

"Well, for starters, what do you do for a living?" He asked.

The dreaded question, Amanda thought to herself as she prepared the light version of her daily task, omitting the job she does at night to make ends meet. "I take care of my son full time; he's sick," she answered, working to not let her emotions show.

"Oh, okay, gotcha."

As if knowing the subject was a touchy one, Amanda was relieved that her date swiftly moved the conversation in another direction. "Well, I'm a lawyer. I just passed the bar a week and a half ago, so this is sort of a celebratory dinner," he said with a flamboyant smile.

Amanda smiled back, enjoying the deep dimples that he displayed with each smile. "Wow, that's great! Congratulations!"

"Thanks, Ms. Lady. I have my first case on Monday. It's a small case and my mentor will be there with me so it shouldn't be too bad."

Yes, a lawyer! I am sitting across from a lawyer. A dude with some real money. A real man with a real career.

"I'm sure you will do fine."

"Yep, me too."

You are selfish. You out with some dude and your son is over here crying, Mandy.

66

Looking down at her chirping phone, Amanda frowned when she saw "no caller ID" display on the screen where there should be a number and an unwanted message from her ex. *How does he know I am out and how the hell does he know this number? I just got this phone. So, he can call and text me, but I don't have his number. Why is he bothering me? How does he even have my number? I just got this phone, and nobody has this number except for Tracy.*

"Is everything alright?"

"Um, yeah. Dorian, I need to make a quick phone call," she said before getting up from her seat.

"Of course," Dorian said with a sweet smile. "Take your time and I will go and take care of the check."

Amanda smiled and waited until her date was out of earshot before she reacted to the message. Sitting back down in her seat and looking again to be sure that Dorian was across the restaurant, she frowned. Tapping the text message, she pushed buttons on her phone. Hoping that a number would magically display in its rightful spot but there was nothing. "No caller ID" still sat in the space, infuriating her.

Hoe.

Squinting her eyes at the text, she balled her right fist up as she held the phone with her left. *Why does he keep texting me from a private number!*

Throwing her phone back into her purse, she faked a smile as Dorian approached the table.

"So, are you ready to go, Ms. Lady?"

"Oh, yes, I need to get home and take care of my son," she lied.

Allowing Dorian to take her hand, she worked diligently to relax as her gracious date led her out of the restaurant.

10

ames! Open this door, I know you're in there!"
Amanda yelled at the top of lungs. Peering through
the front window, she only saw darkness in the living
room. "Coward… talk all that shit in a text but can't
face me," she said under her breath as a few porch lights began
to flicker on from surrounding neighbors. Deciding to try once
more, Amanda walked back onto the porch and rang the
doorbell again, trying to remain calm as she waited for someone
to appear from the darkness and open the door. At the same
time, being careful not to give the neighbors something to talk
about. Taking a frustrated sigh, she slowly walked off the porch
towards the main street to flag down a cab.

"What a night, what a fuckin' night. I go from sitting across the table at a fancy restaurant, eating rich people food with a man who is Idris fine to crazy ass text messages from my bitch ass baby daddy." Amanda mumbled as she hopped out of the cab and proceeded towards her apartment. How can my night turn from great to ridiculous in a matter of seconds?" She continued as she fumbled with her keys. "Oh, come on. Where the hell are they? Why does it always take me forever to get the right key? It's too cold out here tonight for this," she grumbled. Digging into her purse further, she stopped as she thought she heard something or someone fumbling around her area. Hearing nothing but a slow wind breeze, she continued her search for her keys. The rustling of the small bush stopped her in her tracks again. Snapping her head from her purse to the side of the steps, she listened closely. The street lacked adequate lighting and the one light that sat on the apartment's porch was smashed out by the so-called neighborhood gang a few days earlier. Another quick rustling of the bush startled her. Turning sharply towards the sound, Amanda frowned. "Who's that?!" she nervously called out. Frozen by fear, Amanda stood completely still. Peering closer, she noticed a silhouette against the brick of her building. Forcing herself out of her fright, she sprinted into action. Moving quickly, she reached in her oversized bag and fumbled for the small shiny piece that she now kept with her. Mentally fine-tuning her ears and eyes, she

70

called out again, "I said who's that?!" She shouted with an attitude. Amanda listened intently as she heard more rustling from the bushes. Moving further away from the noise, she prepared herself for a fight. In a blink of an eye, a figure leapt out of the bushes, lunging at Amanda. Screaming, Amanda fired a single shot at the intruder. A loud, agonizing scream pierced the night air, letting Amanda know that the bullet had met its target.

PRESTON

1

"You are so slow, Preston. I have to be at work on time too, you know!"

Preston Dixon shook his head and continued to fumble with his tie. "I hate these things," he mumbled as he flipped and tucked, working diligently to complete his look for the day.

"Preston!"

"I'm coming! Give me a sec, Donald!" he called out to his impatient partner.

"I will fix this in the car," he mumbled before opening the bathroom door.

"Finally! I have things to do today too, you know," Donald huffed.

Preston shook his head and chuckled. "I'm well aware of that, Don. You've been telling me that all morning."

"Anyway," Donald answered. "Will you be home in time for dinner? I was thinking pot roast. What do you think? Does that sound good to you?"

Preston kept his eyes on the task at hand while Don removed his bathrobe and turned the shower on. "Whatever you choose

75

to cook, it is your night," Preston answered while brushing his hair. "I will be a little late, though. I am going to see Jordan tonight after work so put my plate in the microwave for me."

Preston waited for his partner to respond. "Don?" he called out.

"I heard you. I just don't think it's a good idea. I mean, why do you keep going over there if your baby mama gives you so much hell all the time?"

Preston eyed himself once more in the mirror before heading out, not bothering to answer Don and then he would be late for work due to yet another senseless argument.

"I will see you later, Don!" he yelled as he walked out into the hallway and towards the front door. Looking in his bedroom, he shook his head at the made-up bed and the clothes folded that was placed neatly on his side. *He always cleaning up something. The day just started and he's already cleaning up.* Grabbing his briefcase from the table in the hall, he tossed it onto his right shoulder and headed out to begin another workday. Stepping out onto the porch, he looked down at the grass, noticing that it was time to cut it. *I guess I better do it this weekend before Don kicks my ass.* Preston and Donald are nothing alike. The saying "opposites attract" really is put into context with the two of them. Donald is the all-around pain in the butt neat freak. If you google the definition for neat freak, Donald's picture should be what's found in the definition's place. Preston, on the other hand is remiss. No, he isn't filthy, he just didn't give as much care to cleanliness as his lover did. Donald is an incredible cook; five-star chef kind of cook. On his nights, he is known for cooking foods that are usually featured on cooking shows and award-winning magazines. Preston did his part by throwing some meat on the George Foreman grill, opening a few cans of vegetables, and dinner was done. Donald is short and stocky. Preston, tall and slim. Donald is bald. Preston has hair that he keeps in waves. You get the picture; they are complete opposites. Walking to his car, Preston smiled at the small batches of pansies that his neighbor found time to plant each and every fall. An array of colors sat immaculately together in each batch, adding a unique beauty to the neighborhood being that she is the only one who took the time to plant anything. Reaching his car, he clicked his key fob and unlocked his doors just as his phone chirped. He sighed and shook his head at the number that was displayed on the screen.

If you are coming over tonight, bring me some wine. Sighing deeply, Preston threw his phone on the passenger seat and briefly planted his head on the steering wheel. "That girl is never going to stop," he mumbled as he started his car. *I don't know why you don't start your car and let the engine warm up,* he heard Donald's voice pestering him. *You're going to mess your engine up.* Chuckling, Preston pulled his head up and leaned it back against the seat. "I'm sure I'll hear his mouth

77

about it tonight. I don't know who gets on my nerves the most at this point, Don or that crazy baby mama of mine." He looked over at his phone and shook his head before throwing his car in reverse and slowly backing out. Slowly driving through his neighborhood, he took the time to enjoy his surroundings. Being the head of the English department at one of Baltimore's most epic universities kept him pretty busy so he didn't have much time to enjoy the outside. Especially since it was early fall, his favorite time of year. He always took extra time during his drive to admire all the beauty and crispness that the fall season had to offer. Smiling, he rolled his window down further to get the first task of the day done, interaction with his people.

"Good Morning, Ms. Benson," he cheerfully greeted the salt-and-pepper haired crossing guard that was posted on the corner of his street.

"Good Morning, Preston. It's a warm day for November, huh?"

"Yes, it certainly is, and I'm enjoying it."

"Yes, me too. Have a good day, son."

"Thanks, you too."

Preston kept his window down as the children of the neighborhood loudly and playfully walked to their usual meeting space before they reached their school. Preston smiled as Ms. Benson waited patiently for the children to get quiet enough so she could recite her daily question.

"Okay, kids; pay close attention," Ms. Benson said. "What do we do before we cross the street?"

"We look both ways!" the children answered loudly and in unison, all of them full of energy.

Preston watched the group of children as they were being led across the street. *One day, Jordan will be a part of that elementary school crowd*, he smiled as he thought of his five-year-old son. Waiting patiently for all the children to reach the other side of the street, Preston pulled out a picture of his son that he kept in his briefcase. "One day, son, you will come and live with me and Don," he said to the picture before kissing it and placing it back in his briefcase. Seeing that all the children crossed the street, he gave one final wave to Ms. Benson before slowly accelerating his car and heading towards Townsend Pines University or TPU as most Baltimoreans called it. Picking up speed a bit, he headed towards the freeway and rolled his window up halfway before clicking the radio on. A dental commercial filled the speakers and he smiled. "Oh shit! My dude finally got an ad on the radio," he chuckled. *Graham's Smile Pediatric Dentistry is now accepting new patients. Call today! Dr. Roger is waiting to transform smiles into Graham's smiles*. Preston laughed aloud. "It's just like Roger to make sure his name is in the commercial." Stopping at the light, he grabbed his phone and began to call his friend. "Nah, I'll call him later tonight. He's probably busy with the kids or getting ready to *transform smiles*." Chuckling, he threw his phone back onto the passenger seat and waited for the light to change. The green light signaled, and Preston quickly went through it, finally making his way onto the freeway. Riding along, he thought of his first class of the day; his best class. *I hope they are ready for my pop quiz. They should be used to them by now.* Pulling his window completely down, he breathed in the soft flow of November's air and made his way through Baltimore's unusually clear beltway.

Townsend, the other side of town from where he lived, was a godsend to him. Preston smiled at a group of students making their way through the streets for their morning jogs and brisk walks. Gorgeous, modern homes and vintage historic buildings lined the streets of Townsend, completed by blissful playgrounds and walking trails. Those were just a few commodities that captivated him and brought him back time and time again. Even when he was off for a holiday, he, along with Don and occasionally Jordan, always found the time to chill in Townsend. The ringing of his phone snapped him out of his bliss, and he shook his head. He ignored the annoying ring tone that he chose just for his son's mother. "Not now, Stephanie," he uttered. S*he knows I'm on my way to work. Watch, her ass will be texting next.* On cue, the phone chirped, alerting him of a new message. Sighing, he turned the corner and entered the professors' parking lot in search for the big jackpot; a close parking space. "Really?!" He exclaimed while quickly pulling his car into the only available space that was directly in front of the faculty and staff entrance. "A good day already! The freeway wasn't full of crazy people all trying to beat each other to an imaginary finish line and the closest and best parking space is free. This doesn't happen every day," he said aloud as he gathered his materials from the passenger seat and hopped out of the car.

"Good Morning, Preston. How are you doing today?"

"Jennifer, good morning," Preston smiled at his co-worker and fellow professor. "I'm well, how are you doing?" Preston smiled as he grabbed Jennifer's books that she struggled to carry.

"Such a gentleman, I like it."

"That, I am. Well, sometimes," he joked and laughed.

"Yeah, sometimes," Jennifer laughed aloud and nudged Preston. "I've seen you act a fool a few times, I already know."

Preston laughed and readjusted the load of books. "So, how are things going? Did you get your microscope fixed yet?"

"Nope, not yet. Still waiting for someone to come up and help me with it. I've been using my personal one until someone answers my email about it. It's like pulling teeth to get Allan to fix something on time."

"Good morning Professor Dixon, Professor Wright."

"Good morning," Preston and Jennifer greeted a mutual student in unison.

"That girl is way too formal," Jennifer mumbled. Why can't she do like all the other students here and call us by our names?"

"Well, she did," Preston chuckled.

"Oh, yeah, professionalism. That's what I get for getting an *English Lit* professor to talk about somebody," Jennifer laughed aloud.

"Oh stop," Preston laughed along with Jennifer as they made their way up the stairs and to the double doors that led to the science hall. Opening the door to the front entrance, they continued with small talk until they reached the auditorium. Holding the door open for his friend, Preston chuckled. "I don't know how you're able to teach in here," he said as he placed Jennifer's book on the small desk.

"Ah, I do my best," she answered while taking her jacket off and hanging it up on the small coat rack. "I mainly do lecture in here and lab in the classroom in the back, so it's not too bad. How's everything going with your classes? I'm sure you have a pop quiz coming up soon."

Preston smiled before answering. "Yup, as-a-matter-of-fact, I have one today," he boasted. "Have to keep the wonderful world of *English Lit* exciting for my students."

"Yes! You do! I guess you gotta' get your day moving and poppin' somehow with that stuff. You are so into it that it makes me sick! Too boring for me."

"Yeah, well, not everybody is in to cutting up frogs' bellies and dissecting cow brains."

"That stuff is where it's at," Jennifer laughed while grabbing a tray of petri dishes off a rack and placing them on the table next to her desk.

"Right," Preston smiled. "Well, let me go and get the day started. I started out with a nearly deserted freeway and a close parking space so, let's see if I can keep the momentum going."

"Yeah and do that by giving the dreaded pop quiz," Jennifer chuckled. "I hear the students talking about them."

"Really, now. Well, that's good," Preston smirked. "That means I'm doing my job the right way," he quipped as he walked towards the doors that led to his hall.

Jennifer laughed while continuing to adjust her materials for her class. "Oh, hey listen! Before I forget again. Jeff and I are doing a dinner party the week before Thanksgiving. I hope you and Don can make it."

Preston turned and smiled at Jennifer. "Thanks for the invite, I'll check with Don and let you know."

"Okay, sounds great. We would love to have you."

Preston nodded his head, in shock that it finally happened. *Nobody has ever invited us to a party or anywhere for that matter as a couple before outside of family. Maybe our relationship isn't a mistake and I made the right choice.* Feeling a small weight release off his shoulders, he happily walked out of the auditorium. Preston greeted more of the students and faculty of TPU before heading to his class to give his pop quiz.

2

W ell, you are finally here. I've waited all day for you."

Preston gazed at his ex-fiancé, in disbelief that she still didn't understand that no meant no and he didn't want to be with her; only have a relationship with her to make it easier for their son. Ignoring her advance, Preston went straight to the point.

"How you doing, Stephanie. Where is Jordan?"

"Our son is upstairs. Come on in and I'll get him for you; after we have a glass of wine together."

Pretending to miss her comment, Preston remained quiet as he walked in the home that was once his and sat down on the couch. "I love the new paint; looks nice," Preston said, attempting to make cordial small talk. Mainly to keep Stephanie's mind from wandering into another rant about his sexuality.

"Thank you, honey. I wanted to spruce up the place a bit."

Preston smiled back, trying his hardest to keep the moment light and to remain on his ex's good side.

"Jordan, come on; your daddy is waiting on you!" Stephanie called out.

"So, where are you taking him today?"

"Well, we will start by going to the arcade and then grab some ice cream. I will have him back before eight," Preston said as he stood to greet his son.

"Oh really?" Stephanie asked with a hint of sarcasm in her voice. It's too cold for ice cream, don't you think?"

"Here we go," he grumbled at Stephanie's comment, knowing full well that she was now in her, what he and Don called, his *get in his ass mode.* In a flip of a switch, Stephanie could turn from the sweetest person in the world to the devil's assistant, and Preston was now in the midst of the change. Thinking of a statement that would counteract her hate, he put his head down. "Aw, it's never too cold for ice cream," he partially cooed. Hoping that his relaxed and loving tone would extinguish her fire.

"I guess not," she softened.

Yeah, calm down. Maybe we can get the hell out of here before she starts it back up. Preston waited impatiently for his son to come down the stairs. He looked around at the same photos on the wall that he always looked at when he was there, just to pass the time quickly and to keep his visits as drama free as possible. *Anything is better than having to chop it up with her.*

"So, you aren't planning to take my baby to see that man you call a boyfriend...are you?"

Damn, I should've known. Too good to get up out of here without dealing with that. Making sure he was as polite as he possibly could be, he looked at Stephanie and pleaded. "Stephanie, listen I—"

"Daddy!"

Thank you, Lord. You sent him down right on time! "Hey son! How are you?"

Preston hugged his son and kissed him on the forehead, grateful for the interruption. "Are you ready for some fun at the arcade?" Preston beamed, particularly enjoying the smile that appeared on his son's face after the mention of the arcade.

"Yeah! And Ice cream!"

"See," Preston looked at Stephanie and smiled. "I told you it's never too cold for ice cream."

Ignoring the look on Stephanie's face, Preston wasted no time to get out of there. He put his son down and grabbed his coat off the chair. "It's warm out today but you still need your coat."

"I know dad. Pneuonia weather."

Preston laughed aloud. "Yeah, son, that's right. It's *pneumonia* weather."

"Right, pneuonia weather."

Jordan looked up at Preston and Preston laughed again.

87

"Close enough, I guess," Preston chuckled.

Taking his son's hand, Preston waved at Stephanie while walking out the door, grateful that he was finally able to leave, with his son in tow and without an argument.

"Hey! What about your wine?" Stephanie yelled.

"No, thank you, Stephanie. I'm driving, remember?" he said coolly, without bothering to look back.

"Okay, well, when you come back. We can have a glass of wine and relax."

Preston chuckled, *this is sad how she begs* "No thanks, I will be dropping Jordan off at eight and then I'm going home," he answered, working diligently not to lose his patience. Preston smiled at his ex before opening the back door.

"Oh yeah, okay Preston. I gotchu'. Let's see how *cool* you are after I get finish sending some messages to your bitch!"

Preston and Jordan both stopped, turned, and looked at Stephanie. Jordan was confused and Preston was beyond pissed.

"Son get in your chair and turn on a cartoon. I'm going to talk to your mom for a minute. Leave the door open."

"Okay."

"And make it a good one!" he called over his shoulder, hoping that his interest in his son's world of cartoons would lighten the soured mood Stephanie put them both in.

Using every bone in his body to stay clam and not to smack her as hard as he could, Preston walked onto the porch and sighed. "Stephanie don't start with your shit today," he spoke softly yet firmly before glancing back at his son and turning to face her. "Don't start that and especially in front of my son."

"Our son and I will say whatever I damn well please."

Frowning, he noticed a look on his ex's face that he didn't recognize. Yes, she has given him some crazy, nasty, and downright hateful looks ever since he broke off their engagement and confessed that he was in love with someone else and that he was leaving her to be with him and to live his life as his true self. This look was a look unlike any of the others; more like a twisted, passionate look. Or maybe even an *I'ma kill you and him look.*

"I'm telling you, Preston, if you don't change back, I promise you that I'm going to make your life a living hell!"

"Change back? What the hell are you talk—"

"Change back to being straight! You know what the hell I mean!"

Preston tilted his head slightly to the left to try to regain his composure. He was standing as if he was calm, but his body burned with anger and he was close to releasing it all, starting with a hard punch to Stephanie's jaw. He kept his balled fist to his sides as he thought of his parents. *Never hit a woman*, his mother has been telling him since he was old enough to fight and his father would follow up with… *Just walk away.* In this moment, he was ready to ignore all that his parents had taught him and deal with the consequences later.

"You heard me! I will call that bitch boyfriend of yours and you *will* change back to being normal."

Preston continued to stand in his misery.

Do it! Smack the bitch…just one good time.

His mind was in a fight of its own at this point.

No, then you will hurt mama. You promised dad that day that you will always protect her. He left that job to you.

Yeah but you will finally feel better and do what you always wanted to do. Smack the bitch.

Preston shook away his thoughts; taking his control of his shoulders away from the imaginary angel on his right one and the devil on his left.

"See, you are starting to act crazy," Stephanie laughed. "Shaking your head and shit. I'm telling you, it's that's dude you messin' with."

Preston turned to look back at Jordan before opening his mouth to speak. "Stephanie, you need to let it go. Listen to me and listen good."

Stephanie folded her arms.

"I do not want you! Move on to somebody else. All I want to do is see my son."

Stephanie laughed loudly, catching Preston off guard. "All you want to do is see your son. Okay, tell you what. How about if I let you see Jordan every single day?"

Preston put his hands in his pocket and waited for Stephanie to continue. A cold breeze whistled in the distance, causing the air to produce a chill.

"I'll even take you off child support. How does that sound?"

"Uh-uh, Preston shook his head. Nope, you know I ain't stupid. You take me off child support and then I don't have any proof that I take care of my son. Then you can go to the judge and lie. Nope, not gettin' me like that."

"Dad! You are missing it!"

Preston turned to Jordan and smiled. "Okay, I'm coming! Just make sure you tell me everything that I've missed!"

"K."

"Your choice, Preston."

Preston turned back to Stephanie and chuckled. "My choice? So, I guess you will let me see Jordan every day and take me off child support if I leave Don and be with you, right?"

"Yes!"

"No, not happening."

Preston turned to walk away but was stopped quickly in his tracks at what Stephanie said next.

"Okay, you can have us both! A marriage is about compromise, right? Let's use those invitations that I have upstairs. The date at the church is still free and my mother still has her mother of the bride dress. I love you that much Preston. I love you so much, that I will let you have Don and me at the same time."

Preston remained with his back to Stephanie, knowing that if he was to turn around, it was a chance that he would walk up to her and the devil from his left shoulder would win the argument with the angel on his right. *She's crazy as hell.* Walking towards his car, he kept quiet, not sure on how he got hooked up with Stephanie in the first place. Yes, his parents wanted hm to live life the *right* way, so he went on his quest to find the perfect woman to bring home to them; to make them happy. It was a time for him to put away his own feelings so that his parents wouldn't be embarrassed in front of their family, mainly their church family. Fate is what his mother called it when he and Stephanie met at the church picnic. "I'm ready for some grandbabies," came next soon after they started dating, and finally, "you got to do things the Christian way," when Stephanie became pregnant and that created the engagement. All happening within six months. *Now, Stephanie is a part of my life forever. Her and all her craziness.* Picking his feet up to walk, he continued to keep his mouth shut as he finally reached the driver's side of his car. Opening the door, he was greeted with Stephanie's wildest words to date.

"Threesome! Bring Don over and you get to have both of us at the same time!"

"Close your door son," he said before putting his car into reverse and backing out of the driveway of horrors.

94

3

*P*reston, was sup, how's everything going?"

Preston smiled at his older brother, Leon. "All good, man. How are you? How's the family doing?"

"Everybody good. Doing good. The girls are in the kitchen helping ma with the crab cakes. Deborah is upstairs with Madisyn, gossiping."

"Yeah, always talkin' bout somebody," Preston chuckled. "How's the baby? Any progress?"

"A little. We are hoping he can come home soon; maybe by Christmas."

"Okay, good." Preston tilted his head towards the stairs, making sure the coast was clear from Deborah. Deborah still struggled with the fact that her brand-new baby boy was born nearly ten weeks earlier than expected, causing him to have to stay in the NICU ever since he's taken his first breath; his very weak breath. Any mention of the hospital brought Deborah to tears and Preston to sadness, so he kept questions about the entire ordeal to a minimum.

"Let me go in here and see mama and the girls."

"Ight man."

Stopping mid-way, Preston smiled at the pictures that lined the wall in the hall that led to the kitchen; what he liked to call his mama's pride and joy wall. Pictures of each member of the immediate family were there; including a picture of the newest member of the family with machines surrounding him and all. The captured moments of when he, his brother, and his younger sister, Madisyn were kids were also there, front and center. Yep, Preston's mom was the queen of photos and she had a decade's worth to prove it; most of them being in her chest in her bedroom. Anytime Preston wanted to take a trip down memory lane, he knew exactly where to go; his mother's bedroom. Fixing his eyes on a picture of his father, Preston's mind wandered to the last day he saw him before prostate cancer claimed his life.

Always take care of your responsibilities, son. Never leave your responsibilities in the hands of others to take care of; take care of your own business. And don't forget to always take care of your mama and your sister. It's in your hands now so make me proud. I love you, son.

From that moment and moving forward, he honored his father's wish and became the sole protector of his mother's home. At first, he struggled with all the responsibility that was put in his hands by the one man he revered more than anyone else in the entire world. *I can't do it*, he would say aloud on many of his tearful nights of missing his father. *It's no way I can take care of mama and Madisyn like he did.* Once he would get himself together and the tears stopped, he would stick his chest out and a great sense of pride would take over. Almost like his father's soul was stepping into his body, transforming him. *Pops trust me so I got to. I'm the man of the family and I'm going to do it.* Although Leon was the oldest child, Preston knew full well that his father wasn't going to trust him, the one who would steal everything in his mother's house when he was on one of his cocaine binges so, he took his father's last request seriously and have been his mother and his sister's protection form the world; from the difficult. Preston fought back tears as he thought of his father's last words to him. Fixing his face into a smile, he walked into the kitchen to greet his mother.

"Hey, what's going on? How are you doing?" he cheerfully spoke, working to hide his lingering grief for his father.

"Hey baby! God bless you."

Leaning in, he hugged his mother tight and gave her a quick peck on the cheek.

"Hi Uncle Preston," both of his nieces said in unison as they ran to hug him too.

"Slow down, girls!" his mother reprimanded. "What did I tell you about running in my kitchen?"

Ignoring their grandmother, his brother's daughters continued to hug Preston while engaging in horseplay all at the same time.

"April and Shayla, what did your grandmother tell you?" Preston joined his mother with the chastising. "Go outside and play; get your energy out that way," he said to the girls. Preston chuckled as he watched his nieces sprint out the backdoor like they were going out there to catch a pot of gold.

"It sure smells good in here, ma." Preston smiled as he went through his rounds of food tasting; opening each pot on the stove and tasting each dish. "Tastes good too," he commented as he replaced the last pot's top and sat down at the table.

"Thank you, baby, but I will break your hand if you go back into my pots. You know I don't play that," she laughed.

Ms. Annie Dixon was the sweetest woman in the world, but she would knock somebody out for going into her pots while she was cooking.

"Yeah, yeah, I know. But you know how I gotta' taste some ma. Can't be waiting until it's all done."

"Uh huh. So, how's everything going son? How's everything going at the school?"

"Everything's all good I'm thinking about starting a tutoring program for those who need extra help. My students know they can come to me anytime, but I think I need something stable. You know, for those who don't like to ask for help but for the ones who will feel more comfortable with more of a structured environment."

Preston and his mother often jumped into conversation about teaching being that they both chose it as their professions. The family called it their *school bell rock* time and would often tease Preston because his words would change ten octaves from the relaxed conversation he had with others who weren't teachers. Words such as *structured* and *environment* were just a couple of the words they all laughed about.

"Oh yes, that would be great, Preston," Ms. Annie answered as she flipped her southern fried catfish. "You know, back in my teaching days at Langston Elementary, I had an after-school tutoring session every week."

"Yep, I remember that."

"I miss being a teacher," she said while placing the cover back onto the pan. "Nothing like shaping the minds of children; especially first graders. First grade is where it all begins with kids. Reading… math… all the good stuff!"

Preston watched his mother as she fumbled with seasonings and utensils, trying to use her arthritis-stricken hands to the best of her ability.

"Speaking of sharp minds, how's my grandson?"

"Jordan's fine. I took him to the arcade yesterday."

"Oh, that's good. You need to bring him by here to see his grandmother."

"I will, Ma, just a lot going on with his mother. You know how that it is."

"Yeah well, I'm going to keep my thoughts to myself about her."

Preston chuckled in shock. "That's a first," he mumbled. "I'll try to bring him over for Sunday dinner this Sunday."

"Okay, I would love to see him. He hasn't had any of my sweet potato pie in a long time. I'll make him one so make sure you get him over here."

I don't know how I am going to do it, but I will somehow, Stephanie will have a fit if she knows that I plan to bring Jordan and Don over here for dinner at the same time; sharing the same space.

"Son help me get dinner onto the table, please. Grab one of the pans for me."
Snapping out of his thoughts, Preston obliged his mother and grabbed the glass casserole dish filled with backed macaroni and cheese, quickly walked in the dining room and sat it in the center of the table.

"Girls, it's time to eat! Come on in and wash your hands!" his mother called out from the back door.

"Madisyn! Deb! Ya'll come on so I can say prayer!"

"Leon, come on in here and help your brother set the table please."

Preston smiled as he listened and watched his mother go into full mother mode. Just as always, she made a point to call everyone in for dinner; starting off with prayer and then sitting down to a delicious, often cooked with a southern drawl, dinner.

4

"ow much did you say the electricity bill is for this month, Don?"

"I don't know; I think two hundred. I will double check."

Preston sat at his kitchen table, sorting out the month's bills. "Two hundred and ten dollars," he said aloud as he looked at the previous month's electric bill. "I sure hope it's cheaper this month, Don. We have to figure out how to get this bill down."

"Yes, you're right, babe," Don said as he placed the current's month bill on the table.

"One hundred and sixty-two dollars," Preston read aloud. "Finally, under two hundred dollars. Opening his checkbook, he happily wrote a check for the bill's amount and added it to his balance in the checkbook.

"I will add my half to your account tomorrow," Don said as sipped his tea.

"Ight. Well, that's it, I just wrote the last check for this month's bills."

"Are you sure, Preston? I think you're forgetting your child support," Donald said as he stood up to refresh his nearly empty cup of tea.

"Nope, I've taken care of that for this month, so we are good."

Donald smiled while pouring more tea into his cup. "Hmm, well, I know the bitch. I'm sure she will call you for something else. Keep your check book open for a few more days before you holler *victory* in the bill paying fight."

Preston chuckled and shook his head. "Good point but I think she's good for now. I just bought Jordan some new sneakers for P.E and some new pajamas. And that was right after I paid the child support."

"Okay, if you say so."

Preston chuckled as he finished the last of his business with his checkbook.

"How is Jordan doing? That old jealous mama of his poison his mind against me yet?"

"Not yet, but I'm sure she's working on it."

Donald shook his head, leaned against the counter, and sipped more of tea. "Yeah, I bet."

Sensing an argument, Preston stood up from the table and quickly walked out.

"How you just going to leave when we are talking?"

"Cause, you are ready to start some shit about Stephanie and I don't feel like dealing with that right now."

"No, not getting ready to start nothing. I just don't understand why you keep dealing with her. The relationship is over so why do you keep talking to her?"

"I deal with her because I have a son with her," Preston yelled before flashing the *end of discussion* glance at Donald and walking into their bedroom, closing the door behind him. Grabbing his laptop and sitting down on the bed, he opened his workstation and sighed. "I don't know who fucks with me the most out of those two. Stephanie with all her wild and crazy ass fantasies or Don's insecure ass. I'm bout ready to pack up all my shit, get my son, and get the hell out of here. Leave both of their crazy asses alone." Adjusting his pillow, he kicked his shoes off and propped his feet up on the bed before grabbing his durag and slipping it on his head. Beginning his routine, he opened his email to check to see if he had any questions, comments, or concerns from any of his students. Skimming through the list he opened one from a student from his honors class. "Shelly," he smiled. "I knew I could count on you with a question." Chuckling, he quickly typed in a response to his student's question and hit the send button. Continuing to comb through his list, he found the usual staff meeting messages and a few holiday event announcements before coming across an unusual looking header. The title read "OPEN

IMMEDIATELY! and was in big bold red letters. "Stephanie," he muttered. "Damn, just let it go; let me go. I ain't never known a woman to be so into one man. All those dudes out there she can get with it and she still stuck on me." Knowing that he shouldn't open it, but delete it instead and keep it moving, curiosity got the best of him. Looking at the door and then back at his screen, he internally weighed his options. *Open it and be pissed off until I go to sleep at the stupid shit she sent. Or, delete it, keep it moving, and take a break from the wack stuff.*

Chuckling, he readjusted himself on his bed and clicked the message.

GET RID OF HIM OR ELSE! spread across the screen in all caps in a bright red font color. *Really, Stephanie.* "You could've at least changed the color from the original *red*." The email became a big blank space as he continued to move his cursor further on the page. "A waste of my time and yours. Instead of sending me messages, why don't you spend more time for Jordan?"

Preston quickly closed his laptop as Donald walked into the room. *Both of them at the same time, hell no.*

"Preston, I… what's wrong."

Preston looked over at Don, being sure to display a look of contentment so any chance of more of an argument would diminish and he could go to bed headache free for the first time in a week. "Nothing, just checking to see if I have any emails from any of my students. Wassup?"

"Just wanted to let you know that I was heading out to the store. You want anything?"

"Nah, I'm good."

Preston waited patiently while Donald changed his shoes from his slippers to his sneakers.

"Be right back."

Donald walked out of the room and Preston waited until he heard the front door close before reopening his laptop and reading the words that were spread across the bottom.

"Oh, and by the way, this is not from Stephanie," he read aloud. *Typical, the ole identity game.* Preston laughed as he clicked out of the message. Deciding not to respond, he opened the first essay and began to grade it.

5

Opening his eyes, Preston looked over at the clock. One forty-five displayed in big bold red numbers. Adjusting his eyes, he fumbled with the contents on his nightstand, trying to find his ringing phone. Grabbing it before the ringing stopped, he breathed "Hello" into the phone, still hoarse from his deep sleep. "Hello?" he muttered again into the phone. "Damn," he quipped as he clicked the off button and placed the phone back onto the nightstand.

"Who was that?" Donald asked in a whisper.

"I don't know; they didn't say anything," Preston said as he yawned.

Turning over, Preston maneuvered his body into a comfortable position. Pulling his pillow under his head, he closed his eyes and prepared himself for more sleep. "What now?" he said aloud as his phone chirped. Sitting up, he grabbed his phone and read the message that displayed on the screen.

Why are you in bed with him? You should be home with me and your son.

Taking a deep, cleansing breath, Preston decided not to respond back. Instead, he turned his phone off and closed his eyes; hoping to get at least four hours of sleep if nothing else.

"Clearly, you got my message last night, Preston."

Preston stood still, almost in a state of shock mixed with panic as Stephanie stood in the middle of his driveway.

"Stephanie, what are you doing here?" he asked in a cold tone. "We have an agreement."

Preston watched Stephanie as she moved closer to his front door, closer to him.

"What agreement? I don't know what you're talking about."

"You know exactly what I'm talking about, Stephanie. You're not supposed to come to my house; the house that I share with Don!" he said, a bit too loudly.

"The house you share with Don," Stephanie mocked. "Well, I am the mother of your child and I should be able to come here anytime I want."

Preston stared at Stephanie, choosing to remain quiet.

"If you want to keep spending time with Jordan, then I suggest you act like you have some sense."

"Stephanie, please leave. I have to go to work, and I am running late as it is," he pleaded.

Stephanie laughed loudly. "I'm not going anywhere until I'm good and damn ready to go!" she answered. "You can't make—"

"Shhh! Lower your voice," Preston interrupted, looking back at the door.

"Why? You don't want your little boyfriend to know that your son's mother is here?"

Preston smiled as he waved at his neighbor. "Good Morning, Ms. Mary," he called out. "How are you doing today?"

"Good Morning, Preston," his neighbor responded while grabbing her newspaper.

"You can't speak to me?" Stephanie harshly blurted out to Preston's neighbor.

The elderly neighbor frowned and shook her head and headed back into her house.

"Stephanie that was uncalled for."

"Well, I am standing here too. She could've spoken to me."

"Look Stephanie, I really need—"

"Why is she here?" Donald asked, interrupting Preston's plea.

111

"Well, well, well, look who decided to come out and join the party," Stephanie sarcastically said as she rolled her eyes.

Preston put his head down and Donald had a look of pure disgust on his face.

"Donald, let me explain something to you," Stephanie said with a hint of anger in her voice. "Preston and I belong together. We have a five-year-old son together who needs both parents in the same house. You do understand that, right?"

Preston sighed and continued to keep his head down. *I wish she would just leave*, he thought to himself.

"Um, Stephanie, I am well aware that you two share a son but that's all you share," Donald calmly responded. "Now, I suggest you get off our property before I call the police."

Preston looked up, glancing around to see if more neighbors had come out to catch a glimpse of the drama that was unfolding.

Stephanie laughed loudly. "I'm not going anywhere. Not until I talk some sense into my baby daddy's head."

"Okay, have it your way," Donald said. "The police will escort you off my property." Donald pulled his phone out of his pocket, placing his keys onto the porch swing.

In a blink of an eye, Preston watched Stephanie leap onto Donald, turning into a woman possessed, kicking and thrashing around.

"Stephanie, stop it!" Preston yelled but his words did nothing to solve the problem.

Stephanie proceeded to punch Donald until he lost his balance and fell against the porch railing. Grabbing her, Preston pulled as hard as he could, trying not to hurt her in the process.

"Get off him, Stephanie!" Preston yelled but Stephanie continued to kick, bite and scratch Donald. Pulling with all he had in him, Preston tugged once more, finally freeing Donald from his attack. *Pulling her off was like pulling a thousand bricks up all at one time*, he thought to himself as he held Stephanie down.

"What is wrong with you, girl?!" Preston shouted as he continued to hold his grip.

"Don, are you alright?"

Jumping up to his feet, Donald used his hand to wipe blood off his face.

"Oh damn, Don! We need to get you to the hospital!" Preston exclaimed, hurt by what he saw.

"You are crazy, Stephanie! I can't believe you!" Preston yelled as he tightened his grip.

"Let me go, Preston!"

"No, I'm holding you until the police come."

"Don, call the police!" he called out as Donald opened the door and went into the house, not saying a word to either Preston or Stephanie.

"What is wrong with you?! You have lost your mind!" Preston yelled.

"This is your fault, Preston. I mean, all you had to do was leave him alone and come home to me and Jordan. I don't ask you for much."

Preston felt the urge to smack the mother of his child, but he was always taught not to hit women. "Girl, you lucky I don't hit women," he said in a whisper.

"You hit me if you want to and I will have your ass thrown in jail."

Preston looked around, noticing that neighbors were standing on their front porches, trying to get a glimpse of the commotion that was taking place. *Take control of the situation, Preston,* he mumbled to himself. Starting with his closest neighbor and the closest person he had to a friend in the neighborhood, he called out to Ms. Mary first.

"Everything is okay, Ms. Mary!" he yelled loud enough so she could hear him.

"Are you sure, Preston? Do I need to call the police?"

"No, it's okay, I promise," he answered as he forced a smile. Everything is under—"

"Yes! Miss! you need to call the police, I'm being threatened," Stephanie interrupted.

"Shhh," Preston muttered angrily.

114

"No, Ms. Mary, don't call the police. Everything is under control."

"Are you sure, Preston? I can get you some help."

"It's okay, Ms. Mary, I've called the police already!" Donald yelled as he walked out of the house.

"Don, are you okay?" Preston asked with a hint of sadness in his voice.

"No, I'm not okay but I will be as soon as I press charges on this harlot you call your son's mother," Donald cried.

"Harlot! Who you callin' a harlot? I got your harlot!" she screamed as she worked to get out of Preston's grip.

"Let me go, Preston!"

"Here they are now," Donald said calmly.

"Over here!" he called out and waved his hands towards the police officers.

The police car stopped as two officers quickly hopped out and walked swiftly towards the porch.

"Sir, do you need an ambulance?" the short, stout officer asked.

"No, I will drive myself to the hospital, but thank you," Donald responded.

"What exactly happened, sir?" the tall red-haired officer asked as he stepped on the porch to further examine Donald.

"That woman attacked me officer and I want to press charges!" Donald said quickly.

"Sir, did you witness what happened?" the stout officer asked Preston.

"Yes, sir, I did," Preston reluctantly answered as he released his confinement grip that he had on Stephanie.

I hate to have my son's mother put in jail, he thought to himself as the police officer pulled his notepad out of his pocket and began to write.

"Okay, and your name, sir?"

"I'm Preston, Preston Dixon," he answered, anxious to get the mini interrogation over and done as quickly as possible.

"I'm Officer Jones," the red-haired officer introduced himself to Donald. "The other officer is my partner, Officer Washington."

Preston watched as the police officer and Donald exchanged pleasantries as he waited for the entire process to run its course. Looking around, Preston noticed more neighbors standing around, cell phones in hand, trying hard to get a good look and clear cell phone footage of the drama that was taking place.

"What ya'll looking at?!" Stephanie yelled loudly.

"Ma'am put your hands behind your back; you're under arrest," Officer Washington said in a monotone as he placed the handcuffs firmly around Stephanie's wrists.

"Under arrest?! For what?!" Stephanie hollered.

Preston put his head down and remained quiet as Stephanie went into another rant.

116

"Assault ma'am," Officer Jones answered with a tone a bit more forceful than Officer Washington's.

"Okay, sir, I have your statement and we will take her in."

"Thank you, officer," Donald said. "I appreciate your help," he continued as he nodded and dapped a towel over his bloody wounds.

"Make sure you get that checked out right away, okay?"

"I will, Officer Jones and thanks again," Donald replied.

Both officers nodded at Preston as they escorted Stephanie off the premises. Preston's eyes followed the officers intently, never taking his eyes off them. *I don't want them to hurt her*, he thought to himself as he watched them carefully place Stephanie in the back of the car.

"Hello? Are you going to go with me to the hospital or are you going to continue to watch your baby mama as if I am not standing here?" Donald asked sharply, snapping Preston out of his thoughts and his gaze.

"Uh, yeah, of course I am going to go to the hospital with you, Don. What the hell kind of question is that?"

"I don't know. Looks like I might have to leave so you can get wit' your nasty ass baby mama one more time before you finally pay me some damn attention. I'll flag the police down before they go so they can bring her back up here, just for you."

Preston looked at Don with a face full of confusion and aggravation; aggravation being the most dominate

117

Shaking his head and rolling his eyes, Donald walked into the house.

"What the hell?" Preston chuckled and smoothed his hand over his head.

Getting his phone from his briefcase, he began to dial his supervisor's phone number when Jordan's picture fell out. "Oh shoot! Jordan!" he said aloud. *I need to get Jordan from school while Stephanie is in jail.*

"Okay, I'm ready."

Preston looked up and then back down towards the ground to retrieve the picture before quickly lifting his head up to do a double take. *Now, I know his ass did not go in the house to beat his own ass.*

"What?!"

Yep, he did! He is just as crazy as Stephanie. Damn, how the hell did I get a messed-up man and a blanked-out woman at the same time? "Nothing, I was just... Come on, let's go." *Nothing I can say about that. That's some crazy shit to go and add more marks on your body just so you can make it look worse than what it really is.* Keeping his thoughts to himself, Preston hopped into Don's car and sat back in his seat, not giving the fiasco with Don and Stephanie any more thought. Instead, he dialed his supervisor's number and thought of the fastest way to beat the afternoon traffic that led to Jordan's school.

6

*U*h, hi. I'm here to pick up my son, Jordan; Jordan Dixon." Preston stood at the front desk of his son's school, nervous about being there as it was his first time picking him up since he's transition over to what Jordan called his "big boy" school.

"Your name, sir?" the slender fair skinned women asked as she pulled out a clipboard and a pen from her desk.

"I- I'm Preston, Jordan's dad," he answered with a smile.

"Oh, okay, sign your name on the clipboard please. I will also need a picture ID unless it's already been scanned into our system. Last name Dixon too?"

"Yes ma'am."

Preston pulled his wallet out of his back pocket and grabbed his driver's license out of the snug space he kept it in. "Here you go," he said as he placed the license on the counter.

"Okay, Mr. Dixon, have a seat and I will send someone to get Jordan for you," she smiled.

"Okay, thanks," Preston replied as he sat down on the burnt-orange chair. Eyeing the interior, he noticed three large potted plants sitting by the massive window behind the large counter. *I like the color pattern in here, burnt orange and purple, nice*, he thought quietly. M*aybe I should paint the living room this color.*

"Ms. Adams?"

The chatter and clatter of a classroom full of students going on with their school day rang out through the speaker as the office assistant waited for a response.

Snapping out of his decorating thought pattern, Preston listened as the fair skinned woman and Ms. Adams exchanged words through the intercom system.

"Yes?"

"Could you please send one of your students down for a sec? Kindergarten shadow pickup."

"Sure, Ms. Adams replied before the assistant clicked the button off."

"I don't believe I've ever seen you before," the fair skinned woman said with a bright smile. "My name is Angela by the way."

"Nice to meet you, Angela."

"Jordan's mother usually picks him up. Is everything okay?"

"Uh, yeah, everything is fine," Preston lied.

It's no way I can tell her that Stephanie is in jail and I was the one who help put her there. "I just thought it would be cool if I picked him up today. You know, give mom a break."

122

"Oh, okay. That's nice," Angela said as she fingered a yellow piece of paper attached to a clipboard. I don't see your name. Your name isn't on his list."

"Excuse me?" Preston frowned and stood up.

"Hmm, you should be on the list," Angela said as she moved the clipboard to the side and typed in some information into the computer. Surveying the computer screen, she squinted her eyes. "I'm looking, and I don't see a Preston Dixon on this list. Um, let me check one more place," Angela said. "Maybe Ms. Gibson forgot to add you or something."

"Yeah, maybe so," Preston said in a tone above a whisper. *How could she not add me to my son's school list? Why did I get hooked up with her? Out of all the females around, I had get wit' her.*

"Excuse me." A little girl holding a small sign that said helper on it, brushed past Preston.

"Hi, Ms. Angela. Ms. Adams sent me here to go and get a kindergartener."

"Okay, sweetie; hold on for a sec," Angela smiled.

Preston watched as Angela looked through a stack of papers on her desk. "No, your name isn't up here either. I'm sorry Mr. Dixon—"

"Preston is fine. No need to be so formal."

"Okay, I'm sorry *Preston,* but I can't allow you to take Jordan if your name isn't on his list of authorized persons."

"Um, okay, ight," Preston responded, beginning to become both angry and embarrassed.

"I do have a Ms. Janet Freemont listed here; Jordan's grand—"

"Grandmother," Preston finished Angela's sentence.

"Yes, his grandmother. I can call her to pick Jordan up if Ms. Gibson is unavailable."

"Hey sweetie, go on back to class and tell Ms. Adams that I said never mind. I will call back if needed."

"K"

Preston moved swiftly to open the door for the class helper. "Have a good day and thank you," Preston smiled.

"You're welcome," the little girl responded with a beaming smile of her own.

"So, would you like me to call Jordan's grandmother?"

Preston turned towards Angela and smiled. "Yes, please. I'm going to go, so could you let her know that Stephanie can't pick him up today. I will call her later to explain."

"Oh, okay. Have a good day, Preston."

"Thanks, you too," Preston said as he opened the door to exit the office.

Preston looked out at the pounding rain from his bedroom window. "It is really coming down out there," he mumbled.

"You better get away from that window before lighting strikes you."

Preston turned and smiled at Donald. "That would be the last nail in the coffin. I had a terrible day today and lightening striking me would definitely not make it any better," he chucked a peaceful and inviting chuckle, in hopes that he would soften any mood Donald was in before he even got started with any rants or complaints.

"A terrible day? What? You mean because you watched your baby mama beat me down and you did nothing?" Donald sarcastically questioned Preston as he pulled the thick black and white blanket back on the king-sized bed.

Well, damn. Keeping his eyes out at the rain, he sighed lightly. "Can we not do that? I already told you that my day was messed up and you still come at me with your bullshit."

"Uh… no… I'm not letting you off that easy. First of all, you allow that ratchet hoe to come all up on our porch; *my* porch. Then you let her jump on me like the rabid dog she is."

"Aye, ight, now you going too far. Stephanie is still my son's mother and I'm not going to let you keep disrespecting her like that."

"Oh… so now you defending the bitch. Oh no…no… not bitch. Don't want you jumping on me and beating my ass so let me redo that."

Preston kept his eyes on the window, making sure to keep his back to Donald, not giving any type of respect by facing him while he's talking.

"You allowed your son's mother to walk on my property and fight me. Is that better? Don't want to *disrespect* her. Nope… don't wanna do that."

Saying nothing, Preston kept his eyes focused on the rainfall, trying desperately to clear his mind.

7

*O*kay, ladies and gentlemen, turn to page twenty-six in your textbook. We will start where we left off on Thursday."

"Uh, Professor Dixon?"

Preston looked toward the sound of the voice and smiled at the student. "Yes, what can I do for you," he asked.

"I'm new here and I don't have my books yet. Do you have one that I can borrow for today?"

"Uh, yeah, Sure," Preston politely answered. "Come on up and I'll get it for you. Oh, and by the way, it's Preston. No need to call me Professor. We are all adults here; we are all on a first-name basis in my classes."

"Oh, okay. Thank you, Preston."

"No problem," he said as he handed her the textbook.

"You might want to switch your class," another student yelled from the back of the room. "My man Preston likes to give us lots of pop quizzes. You are sure to fail this class… at least twice."

The class burst out into laughter.

"Ha-ha-ha! That's funny Travis, but so true," Preston joined in with his class. "Just for that, I might give one tomorrow."

The class quickly changed from laughter to an eruption of boos.

Preston laughed at his class as they continued with their complaints. "All right, okay, settle down ya'll. Chill." Sitting down on the top of his desk and maneuvering into a comfortable position, he opened his teacher's manual of the textbook. "We have a lot of material to cover today. Let's get serious." The class slowly settled down and prepared themselves for the day's lecture.

"Knock, knock. Can I come in?"

"Hi! Of course, Beautiful. Come on in! How's your day going?"

"It's going, lots of lab today," Jennifer rolled her eyes.

"Ah, yes, the exciting world of microbiology," Preston chuckled.

"Tell me about it," Jennifer added. "You know, sometimes, I wish I would've played it safe and mastered in English Lit. Make my job a bit easier."

"You got jokes!" Preston laughed aloud and flopped down in his chair, propping his feet up on a small stool left by one of the custodians.

Jennifer hopped onto Preston's desk and laughed. "You know I had to get that in sometime today."

"Yeah," he chuckled. "But English Lit has its days too, you know. I guess it's all in what you make it."

"Yeah, I guess you're right," Jennifer nodded her head. "If you say so."

Preston shook his head and smiled.

"Hey, did you and Don decide if you were coming to my dinner party? It's next week and I'm still waiting for my answer."

"Oh, yeah, that's right. I have so much going on that I forgot to ask him. I'll ask him tonight." *Shit, if it was up to me, I'd show up with a new man. I don't want to take Don's ass nowhere at this point.* Is anybody going to be there that we should watch out for?"

"What do you mean...? Like who?"

"You know what I mean, Jen. People who got a problem with—"

"You and Don's relationship," Jennifer answered her own question. "Oh Preston, you have to own your life. Who cares what people think or feel about you and Don? It's none of their business and to answer your question... no. Our friends and family don't get down like that. You are free to love whoever you want to love and anybody who has a problem with that, the hell with them."

Preston adjusted himself in his oversized chair. "Yeah, you're right, Jen."

"Yup, I know I'm right," Jennifer smiled.

"It's just people are so mean at times. I mean, they start to treat us different once they find out that we are together and not just roommates. It took our families over a year to get used to the idea and to accept us and my pops went to his grave without giving my relationship with Don a chance."

"Well, that's their problem. Just as long as the people who matter most to the two of you embrace it, then it doesn't matter what others think."

Preston smiled at Jennifer. "Thanks Jen. You are so good to me and for me."

"Yes, I know that," Jennifer joked. "Tell me something I don't know."

Preston stood up and laughed. "You are too much," he said as he wrapped his arms around Jennifer and hugged her tightly.

"I got your back love. I love you for you and whoever you choose to love, well, I love them too. Okay, that's enough." Jennifer pushed back and removed herself out of Preston's emotional, brotherly filled hug. "Enough of the mushy stuff. I expect to see you and Don at my party."

Preston smiled, "Enough said, we will see you there."

Watching Jennifer walk out of his classroom, he leaned against his desk and exhaled. "It's nice to know there are still some good people on this earth." Pushing his chair in further under his desk, he grabbed the dry erase marker and began to write the upcoming assignments on the white board.

"Excuse me, Professor. I- I mean, Preston. Can I come in for a second?"

Preston looked over at the door. "Oh, yes, come in. I don't believe you told me your name earlier," Preston said as he extended his hand for an official greeting.

"Oh, sorry, my name is Heather. Heather Hernandez."

"Oh, okay. Well, it's nice to meet you, Heather."

"Likewise," Heather said in a friendly tone. "I just wanted to return your book."

"Alright, thank you. Did you have any problems getting your books?"

"Well, I haven't picked them up yet. I am having some financial issues, so I won't be able to get them this week. I'm hoping no later than next week though."

Preston smiled genuinely at Heather. "Well, Heather, it's no need to rush. You keep this book as long as you need it."

"Really? Thank you so much, Profe – I mean, Preston."

Preston chuckled. "You are more than welcome, Heather. Please don't hesitate to come to me if there is anything else that I can help you with, okay?"

Heather put her head down before she answered. "Well, there is one more thing," she shyly said.

"Sure, what is it?" Preston sat down on his desk and waited patiently for Heather to ask her favor.

"I was hoping that you could tutor me sometimes… privately. You see, I have trouble understanding material and often need extra help in a private setting. Do you offer a tutoring program here?"

"Yes, we do but I wouldn't mind setting some sessions up just for you, if it helps."

Heather put her head down. "Thanks so much," she said in a light whisper.

"You bet," Preston answered back. *This girl is so shy*, he thought to himself as he continued to watch Heather's mannerisms. *Maybe she suffers from some sort of personality disorder.*

Suddenly, Heather popped her head back up and smiled. "Okay then, just let me know which days and times are good for you," she said in a high-pitched, confident voice, startling Preston.

"Sure," he said quickly. "I will work out some dates and times and get back with you."

132

Like a switch turning off and on, Heather put her head down again and spoke in a shy whisper. "Okay, thank you," she said as she walked towards the door.

Weird, Preston mentally spoke to himself, maintaining the plastered smile on his face.

"Okay then, bye," she said and walked out the door.

Keeping his eyes on the door for a few seconds longer, Preston shook his head. *Something about that girl is off.* "I don't need no more crazy people in my life. Don and Stephanie already filled those slots." Taking a deep, cleansing breath, Preston shook off the feeling of doom that he felt within the pit of his stomach. Turning to the white board, he began to finish the task of creating class assignments for the week ahead.

8

*D*addy!"

"Hey man," Preston stood up to greet his son. "How are you?"

"I'm fine daddy. I want to go to your house."

"Okay, we will see about—"

"Jordan, why don't you go upstairs for a while and play with your new toy grandpa and I bought for you?" Janet, Jordan's maternal grandmother interrupted.

"Okay, Grandma," Jordan reluctantly agreed.

"Daddy, please don't leave, okay?"

Preston kissed his son on the cheek. "Okay son, I won't," he smiled. "Now go and do what your grandmother told you to do."

"Okay, daddy."

Preston and Janet watched Jordan trot up the stairs before either of them said anything to each other.

"How dare you have my daughter thrown in jail?!"
Preston frowned, not ready to have this type of conversation with his ex's mother. Looking in her eyes, Preston saw the

splitting image of Stephanie. Although Janet was aging, you couldn't tell it just by looking at her; she aged beautifully.

"First, don't come at me like that," Preston said as calm as he could. "My son is upstairs, and I don't want to upset him. Second, I didn't have your daughter *thrown* in jail. She came to my house and started wilin' out on my friend. The police came, and they rightfully took her to jail."

Preston eyed Janet, looking for a more understanding look in her face but found nothing but pure anger and rage.

"Preston, you can do whatever you like with your life. You can engage with anyone you choose, but don't hurt my daughter any more than you already have in the process."

Preston shook his head, searching his brain for a response that wouldn't cause the situation to become worse. "Ms. Janet, with all due respect, I'm not the one hurting Stephanie. Stephanie is hurting herself by not coming to terms that she and I are over, and we are not going to get back together."

There was a pregnant pause before he continued.

"Now, I care for Stephanie because she is the mother of my child but that's as far as my feelings go for her." Preston smiled at Janet, hoping that his smile alone would soften her mood.

"I see," she said in a hushed whisper. "Well, Preston. I can't tell that you care for her. If you cared anything about Stephanie, then she wouldn't be sitting in a jail cell, waiting for someone to bail her out."

Preston remained quiet as Janet spoke her mind.

"Now, I am upset with you about all this but there is a way to make it right."

"Uh, okay," Preston slowly said. "How can I do that?" He asked in a polite tone.

"You can give us the money to bail my daughter out and get her home to her son."

Preston chuckled in surprise. "Excuse me?" Preston blurted out, trying to regain his calm composure.

"What is so funny? You laughing at me or my daughter?"

Preston shook his head and crossed his arms. "Janet, I'm not laughing at either of you. I just find your request absurd; that's all."

The chirping of the phone interrupted the awkward conversation that was taking place. Grateful for the interruption, Preston pulled his phone out of his pocket and opened it.

Where are you…? I picked up some food from Dominick's.

Typing in his password, he responded with relief. Relief that the message wasn't full of hate this time like so many of the others that he's been getting over the past week.

I will be home in a minute, he quickly typed in before relocking his phone. Looking up, Preston caught a look of hatred plastered on Janet's face, causing him to want to go out the front door instead of standing in front of her.

"Ms. Janet, listen, I hate because Stephanie is in this mess but there is nothing that I can do."

"Sure, there is. You can get my daughter out of jail!" she yelled.

"Grandma?"

Both Preston and Janet turned towards the tiny voice coming from the direction of the stairs. Jordan stood there with tears in his eyes.

"Why are you yelling at my Daddy?"

"Oh, Son, come here," Preston motioned for Jordan to come closer to him.

Preston walked closer to the stairs and Janet turned away and put her head in her hands.

"Everything is okay. Your grandmother and I are just having a disagreement; that's all."

"Uh, yes, sweetie, that's all," Janet turned back towards Jordan and smiled.

Preston wiped Jordan's tear stained face and kissed him on the forehead.

"I want to go with you Daddy. Can you take me with you?"

Although he hated that he felt the need to get permission to take his son anywhere, he showed respect anyway and looked over at Janet for an answer.

"Well, sweetie, I think you should stay here with grandma and grandpa for tonight," she answered in a soothing tone.

"No grandma, I want to go with my daddy," Jordan cried, the tears flowed rapidly as he spoke.

"Jordan, your grandma is right," Preston painfully agreed. "I know your mommy is going to want to see you when she comes back." Preston kissed his son again and picked him up.

Jordan held on to Preston and Preston squeezed back, not wanting to let him go. "When is mommy coming, daddy? Grandma said she will be here soon, but she is taking a long time."

"Well, son, your mommy—"

"Is taking care of some important stuff," Janet jumped in and Preston sharply looked over at her.

"Don't do that, Janet. Please don't interrupt me when I'm talking to my son," he said with attitude. "I know how to talk to him without upsetting him. I don't need you to help with that."

"Ha!" Janet huffed. "Uh-uh, *Preston*. This is my house and I will interrupt any time I feel the need."

"Hey, why are ya'll down there making all that noise? I can't even hear the TV or my own snoring with all that noise." Thomas, Stephanie's father, called out from the top of the stairs.

His own snoring? And how the hell can he hear the TV if he... the whole damn family is crazy. Preston held in his ridiculing laughter while Thomas waited for an answer.

Preston and Janet exchanged a quick glance at each other before Janet responded to her husband.

"Oh, it's nothing, dear. Preston and I are having a conversation." Janet walked closer to the stairs. "I was just saying goodnight to him, honey."

"Okay, well keep it down. Will ya?!" Thomas replied harshly before slamming his bedroom door.

I need to get my son out of here.

As if reading his thoughts, Janet spoke quickly and much quieter than when their conversation first started. "Jordan is staying here with us tonight and it's getting close to his bedtime, Preston."

Forcing a smile, Preston put his son down

"Jordan, I promise that you will come and spend some time with me, okay? Just not tonight, son."

"Jordan, say goodnight to your daddy. It's time for bed."

Irritated and frustrated, Preston snapped. "Um, just a minute Janet. Now, I already told you..." Sighing, he dipped his head briefly and picked it back up before focusing all his attention on his son's grandmother. "I asked you to stop interrupting me when I'm talking to my son. Now, I know why you're doing this, and I promise you that you nor your daughter will keep me from my son," he said in an extremely calm voice; a voice that nobody in the room recognized, including himself.

Preston lifted his son again and kissed him on the forehead before sitting him on the couch.

"Oh really? Let me ask you this… *professor*. How do you know Jordan is really your son?"

A tremendous feeling of attack; like water invading his lungs gripped Preston like he was in the final moments of his life. In that very second, he knew what it felt like to have your heart ripped out of your chest. The fact that he was hearing the new revelation that Jordan may not be his son, from a reliable source, was too much for him to handle and he knew that he had to get out of the situation before he made a move that he wouldn't be able to take back. Flight or fight and in this case, he couldn't choose the latter.

"Ever think about the fact that he may not even be yours?" Janet continued in a taunting nature.

Preston chuckled, not saying another word to Janet, he turned to his son. "I love you son and I will see you again soon."

"Okay Daddy, I love you too."

"Listen to your grandma and grandpa. Be a good boy, okay?"

Preston smiled at his son before walking out the front door, not saying another word.

9

ark my words! You will pay for what you did to me. Preston read the text message aloud. "Another one," he mumbled as he opened his briefcase and removed his grade book. *That girl needs to get over it already. I will not let Stephanie ruin my evening.* Getting up from the kitchen table, he turned the oven on and opened the refrigerator. Grabbing the ground beef that he prepared earlier, he added a few more ingredients before placing the dish into the oven.

"Preston, come and open this door! It's cold out here!"

"Ma?" he asked aloud as he walked towards the banging and the yelling. Opening the door, he frowned. "Ma, what the heck are you doing over here?"

"I came to find out what is going on with you," his mother answered as she brushed past him.

"How did you get all the way over here?" he asked, while looking around outside before closing the door.

"Your sister brought me over here."

"Um, okay, where is she?" he asked in a confused voice. "She'll be right back; went down the street to the store. We can talk before she gets here," Annie said.

Preston was in a state of shock. It wasn't every day that his mother abruptly came over for a visit.

"Let me take your coat." Preston moved quickly to help remove his mother's coat. "Come on into the kitchen, Ma. Do you want some coffee? Tea?"

"Coffee please, son. I need something to calm my nerves," she said as she sat down at the kitchen table.

Preston swiftly walked over to the coffee pot and began to make his mother her requested drink. "So, what's going on, Ma?"

"Hmph! You tell me. What is this I am hearing about Stephanie and Donald fighting?"

Preston poured his mother's coffee and turned on the oven light before joining her at the table. "Well, to make a long story short, Stephanie came over here and attacked Donald."

Flabbergasted, Annie put her hands over her mouth. "No, Ms. Thang didn't!" she quipped.

Preston chuckled. *It's always funny to hear Ma talk when she's gossiping about something or somebody.*

"Yes, she did. It was like seeing a wild animal go into attack mode. I mean Ma, it was like a rabid animal. I never knew Stephanie was so strong," Preston rested his elbow on the table.

"Of course, she was in that moment," Annie blurted. "You never underestimate a woman scorned, son. Never forget that," his mother warned as she sipped her coffee.

"Preston! I heard your baby mama went ham the other day!"

Preston looked towards the living room to find his sister walking in with a giant smile on her face.

"Hey Madisyn," Preston smiled at his sister. "Do you want something to drink?"

"No, I'm good, bruh but I would like to hear more about what happened with your boy and your baby mama," she shrieked.

Preston shook his head and laughed aloud. "Like I was just telling Ma, Stephanie came over here, Donald came out the house and Stephanie jumped on him," he condensed the story into one sentence. "The police came, and she was arrested."

"Word?! I always knew that chick of yours was crazy. Is she still in jail?" Madisyn asked with excitement laced in her voice.

"No, she must've gotten out sometime today," he answered quickly, thinking back to the unwanted text that he received from her before his family arrived.

"Well, I don't want my grandson around all that devilish mess they got going on over there. All of them people over there are a mess. What are you doing to get him away there?"

Preston stood up and walked over to the oven. "There's nothing I can do, Ma," he said as he turned the oven down and readjusted the timer on the microwave.

"Sure, there is. You are his father. You have rights too," Annie argued.

"That's right, and if you need me to go over there and get him, you know I'm down," Madisyn chimed in.

"I'm sure you will, Maddie," Preston snickered. "You know, I tried to go and get him from school on the day all this happened, and I found out that I am not even on his authorized persons list." Grabbing a coffee mug from the counter, Preston poured himself a cup of coffee and leaned against the counter. "Then," he continued, "I went over to Ms. Janet's house to see him and she wouldn't let Jordan come home with me. Made the excuse that his mother was coming back for him soon, so he should stay there with her."

"Unbelievable," his mother uttered.

Madisyn shook her head and remained quiet.

Preston thought back to the hostile conversation that he had with his son's grandmother, particularly the bit when she questioned Jordan's paternity. *Is there any meaning to it*? he thought to himself, careful not to alert his mother and his sister with that information. *Only one way to find out… a paternity test.*

146

"Speaking of your man, where is he?" Madisyn asked, pulling Preston back into the kitchen with them and away from the sting that his thoughts brought him.

"Donald is still at work," Preston smiled. "Dr. Bright asked him to work late tonight at the after-hour's clinic with so many sick kids here lately."

"Yeah, cold and flu season," Annie jumped in and took another sip of her coffee.

"Yup, a big need for the physician assistants during this time of year," Preston followed.

"You know, I was thinking of following in Donald's footsteps and become a physician assistant. Do you think Donald would give me a few pointers on where to start?"

"Sure, he would, Madisyn. Just ask him to be your mentor," Preston smiled at his sister, happy that she was finally taking an interest in something besides games on her phone and strip clubs. "He'll be glad to do it. It's about time you are getting serious about your career goals, anyway."

"Oh, shut up," Madisyn laughed, flinging a piece of paper at her brother.

Preston laughed, opened the oven and placed the oven mitt on his hand before pulling the rack out just enough to baste his meat. "Ya'll staying for dinner?"

"Smelling good up in here!" his mother smiled.

147

"Thanks," Preston chuckled. "Ya'll know my meatloaf is always on point. Ya'll want some?"

"Oh no baby. Madisyn and I need to get to the store and get some of the food for Thanksgiving dinner." Standing up, his mother kissed him on the cheek. "Love you, God bless you and make sure you stay out of trouble, you hear?"

"Yes ma'am, I hear you Ma," he said as he gave his mother a return kiss on her forehead.

"Bye big head!" He called out to his sister.

"Bye, big lips," Madisyn joked as she walked towards the door.

"Don and I will bring dessert to Thanksgiving dinner."

"Okay baby make sure it's the apple—"

"I know, I know," Preston cut in. "Cinnamon and powdered sugar apple pie form Dominick's. Got it covered," he smiled at his mother.

Annie chuckled, "I should've known, son. You know your mother so well."

"That I do," he agreed.

Preston grabbed his mother's coat and helped her into it. Kissing her again, he opened the door for her and his sister and walked them outside to his sister's car. "Okay, drive safely," he said as he opened the car door for his mother.

"I will," Madisyn called out from the driver's seat. "See you on Thanksgiving," she added.

Preston waited until his sister's car was out of view before heading back into the house.

"I want to thank you again for meeting me. Especially since it's right before Thanksgiving and all."

"Yeah, you're very welcome," Preston smiled. "Always willing to help a student."

"Thanks," Heather smiled and put her head down.

Preston nodded his head slowly and sat down in his chair. "Okay, so you can complete the thesis and the worksheet and that should get you ahead. Don't worry about completing the worksheet this week. I just want you to focus on your family and spending time with them during the Thanksgiving break."

Heather slid her hands under her shirt and smiled, catching Preston completely off guard.

"Um, Is everything—"

"Oh, yeah. My bad," she chuckled. "My hands just get cold a lot, so I tuck them under my shirt."

"Uh, okay."

Preston stood up and moved behind his desk, bringing some added distance between them. Although Heather said she meant nothing by her gesture, Preston felt differently and wanted to get as far away as he possibly could without making her feel a way.

"Alright, so I guess we both should be going," he smiled politely as he quickly grabbed his briefcase.

"Um, yeah."

Walking towards the door, Preston turned back to see Heather standing in the same spot, not making any attempts to move as her eyes were completely fixated on him.

"Heather?"

Heather stood in a trance, not moving a muscle.

"Uh, hello? Heather, are you—"

"Whew!"

Startled, Preston slightly jumped back before putting his hand on the doorknob. *I got to get the hell out of here. Something is wrong with that girl.* "Heather, are you alright?"

"Yeah!" She excitedly blurted out. "Everything is perfect!"

"Um, okay. Do you need anything else before I go?" Preston asked slowly as he was no longer sure if he should continue to stay in his classroom; in her presence.

"Yes, just one thing."

150

Preston glanced at the door and then back at Heather. "What is it?"

"How's Donald doing?"

"Excuse me?" Preston moved his hand completely off the door and focused all his attention on Heather.

"How's Donald?"

Preston stood dumbfounded. Not sure on what to say or how to say it, he just stood in place and waited for Heather to go forward.

"You know, it's been years since I saw him last. He just up and disappeared on me after he killed my father."

A thick wave of dizziness swept Preston like a raging hurricane and his ears began to buzz. "W-what did you just say?" He placed his briefcase on the floor and walked slowly towards Heather."

"If I were you, I would watch my back! That dude is crazy. My dad never saw it coming!"

Every nerve in Preston's body was numb so he couldn't stop Heather as she whipped past him and out the door. Leaning against the wall, an enlarged version of Donald's face burned into his mind. "What the hell was she talking about?" Forcing his body to move, he picked his briefcase up off the floor, slid it on the table that sat beside him, and pulled his phone out. Reaching his contacts, he slapped Donald's number but quickly shut it off. "I need to see him in person," he mumbled. "I need to see his face." Throwing his phone back into his briefcase and closing it tightly, he hurried out of his classroom and to his car, hoping to catch Donald before he left his job.

"Say what now?" Donald frown.

Preston put his head in his hands and sighed. "She said you killed her father. What the hell is going on?!"

"Aye! First of all, you need to calm down. This is a hospital with a bunch of nosey ass people waiting for the next gossip report. I don't need them all up in my business no more than they already are. Come on to the lounge while nobody's there."

The fact that Donald felt the need for privacy worried Preston so much so that it was causing a headache to form over his left temple. Ignoring the pain, the best he could, he waited behind Donald as Donald slid his badge over the door's security scanner. Donald opened the door and Preston followed. His mind was swarming with anxiousness and fear as he waited for Donald to start the much-needed conversation.

"I was eighteen years old," Donald started.

Preston looked at him and waited. Wondering why it took a perfect stranger to tell him something about his partner that he should've told him a long time ago.

"I met Chris at a party right before I graduated high school." Donald looked around the room before he continued. "I was just coming out and he… well, he was still struggling with his identity. You know, being from a big church going family, he had to be careful about his preferences."

Preston kept his eyes on Donald, silently pressing him to continue.

"A few years later, we met up again and this time, he was comfortable about who he was and what he wanted. It didn't make a difference to him, male or female, just as long as the person he was with made him happy. So, we started a relationship. Although he was open and honest with his friends and mates, his family was still kept in the dark. Well, all except for his daughter, Heather. He had full custody of her due to the fact that she was suffering from schizophrenia and her mother couldn't handle her."

Preston's eyes widened. *Everything is finally making sense. The outbursts… the trances… everything.* Deciding to keep her actions to himself, he remained quiet.

"A year or so later, Heather's uncle was released from Prison and found out about me and Chris and that's when all hell broke loose."

"All hell?" Preston whispered, finally having the urge to speak since the conversation started.

"Yeah." Walking towards the door, Donald slightly opened it and peeked out. Seeing that everything and everyone was in order, he closed the door and turned towards Preston.

"Yep, he hated that Chris wanted to be with me. He felt that our relationship was a bad influence on his niece." Sighing loudly, Donald put his head down and shook it slightly. "So, one night, during Chris' jog, Heather's uncle and a few of his boys rushed up on him and kidnapped him at gunpoint."

Preston moved his body uncomfortably as he listened to Donald recount the story. A story that he was sure caused his man great pain. The look in Donald's eyes told it all; that he still held the memory vividly and close to him.

"Those fools forced him in the woods and made him shoot himself. They were too cowardly to do it themselves, so they put the gun in his hand and put another gun to his head and forced him to pull the trigger."

A single tear fell down Donald's face, causing Preston to react. Walking over to him, Preston placed a comforting hand on Donald's shoulder. "Why didn't you ever tell me about this before?"

"It's too painful. I don't like talking about it."

Donald put his head down and Preston rubbed his back.

Chris' family blames me for what happened. They poisoned Heather's mind and turned her against me. So, I walked away and never turned back."

Looking off in the near distance, Preston found a new respect for Donald. He wasn't exactly sure why, he just knew that he did and at that very moment, nothing or nobody was going to ever tear him away from Donald. The relationship was sealed, as far as he was concerned, forever.

*I*t is pouring out there today! Happy Thanksgiving ya'll!" Preston yelled as he walked through the front door.

"Hey Preston! Happy Thanksgiving, man.

"How are you doing, Don? It's good to see you again," Madisyn's boyfriend, Chad said as he stood to greet Preston and Donald.

"Preston!"

"Donald!"

Happy Thanksgiving!" Madisyn cried as she emerged from the kitchen.

"How are you, Donald?" She asked as she exchanged hugs.

"Hey, Madisyn, I'm great," Donald replied.

"Good, I'm glad you made it."

"Uh, excuse me, little sister. I'm standing here too," Preston joked.

"Yeah, yeah, yeah! I see you," Madisyn said as she smacked her brother on the arm and gave him a quick hug. "Please tell me you got mama's apple pie from Dominick's," she said as she grabbed a bag from Preston's hand.

157

"Yes, I got it," Preston answered as he removed his coat. "I don't need to hear mama fussing at *me* on Thanksgiving."

"Right!" Madisyn exclaimed as she walked towards the kitchen.

"Mama? Preston and Donald are here!"

Preston and Donald walked into the kitchen.

"You got it smelling real good up in here Ma," Preston said as he hugged and kissed his mother.

"Thank you, baby. It will be time to eat soon," she replied as she placed her infamous holiday dressing into a baking dish and placed it into the oven.

"How are you doing, Ms. Annie?" Donald shyly asked.

"Hi baby," Annie responded. "It's so good to see you. God bless you."

Preston smiled at the exchange between his love and his mother. Thinking back, he remembered a time when his mother wasn't too fond of Donald. Well, it wasn't Donald, but the lifestyle he and Donald decided to live. Every time he and Donald were both in the presence of his mother, he would think back to those times; a habit that he was still working to break.

Men ought not to mingle that way, son," she would say.

Mama, I am free to love who I want to love," he would tell his mother. *"I love you, but I also love Donald and we want to be together.* Snapping back into the present, Preston smiled as he watched Donald and his mother converse.

"Yes, cinnamon and sugar apple pie!" Annie exclaimed. "I sure do appreciate ya'll bringing it."

Preston smiled at his mother. "You're welcome, Ma. Anything to make you happy," he said as he sat down at the table.

"I know it was crowded at Dominick's today," Annie replied as she wiped down the stove.

"No, it wasn't too bad, maybe because of the rain," Donald jumped in.

"I know, it is really coming down out there," Annie nodded her head.

"Yeah, who would've thought Baltimore would be under a severe thunderstorm warning on Thanksgiving Day?" Madisyn said as she walked into the kitchen and grabbed a dish cloth to help her mother clean. "I could see a snowstorm, but a thunderstorm?" Madisyn walked over to the sink, turned the water on and proceeded to wash the two pans that were there.

"I know, right," Preston commented. "I just hope it turns and go another way."

"Well, whichever way it decides to go, we are going to have a good time and enjoy a good Thanksgiving," Annie smiled as she placed a big dish of candied yams next to the macaroni and cheese in the oven.

"Right, ma," Madisyn said.

"So, is that witch going to let Jordan spend some time with us today?" Madisyn asked in a sarcastic tone.

Donald chuckled and got up from the table. "I'll be in the living room, watching the game."

"I don't know," Preston answered. "You know she's still mad because of what happened the other day."

"Hmm, well, that answers my question then. That girl is not going to let Jordan come over here. Especially if she knows that Donald is here." Madisyn said as she finished the last pot and sat across the table in front of Preston.

"Well, maybe she will act like she has some type of sense and do what's best for Jordan. These women got to stop holding these kids like they are property instead of human beings; stop keeping them away from their daddies just because they are upset with them. It's just not right," Annie said as she sat down to join her children at the table.

"Hell will freeze over before that happens." Madisyn chuckled before quickly getting up and walking out of the kitchen.

"That girl is a mess, but she's right. You know, son, you have rights too. Jordan is as much of your son as he is hers."

Preston put his head down before answering. "I know, Ma. I'm just tired of fighting with her. You know, it's me and her in a relationship or nothing at all," he said. "I mean, the girl won't settle for being just friends. She wants more."

"Yes, son. Unfortunately, these girls today have these babies and use them as pawns. You are going to have to take her to court, Preston. Try to get some sort of custody of your son. Lord knows, I want to see my grandson a lot more than I do, and you need to be in his life a lot more than you are. I know you take up time with him, but you need to be around him every day. Not just when she thinks it's alright."

Preston remained quiet as his mother spoke, knowing that she was telling the truth and wishing that it was something more he could do to make his truth becomes Stephanie's as well.

"It's hard enough that there are lots of kids growing up without the benefit of a father. When you have a man that wants to be around, the law ought to make it so!" she said forcefully.

"Mama don't get worked up. Don't worry yourself about that. I will figure something out," he stood up and rubbed his mother's back, gently consoling her. He grabbed Annie's hand and lovingly squeezed it.

"I'm sorry, son. I just get so mad with women who keep kids away from their daddies just because they are mad about something. The only person to suffer is the child," Annie replied as she stood.

Preston reached down and hugged his mother "It's okay Ma, I will get everything straight," he said softly and kissed his mother on the cheek.

161

"Hey! Happy Thanksgiving!" Deborah, Annie's niece cried out happily as she entered the kitchen.

"Hey Deb! God bless you!" Annie exclaimed as she wiped her eyes.

"What are the sad faces and crying about?" Deborah asked loudly as she hugged her aunt.

"Oh, it's nothing," Annie answered. "Just having a talk about Jordan."

"Oh, ya'll better stop letting that situation get the best of ya'll," Deborah said as she hugged Preston. "If the girl doesn't want the baby around, then forget about it. Jordan will be old enough to make his own decisions soon enough."

"Yeah, I guess so," Preston said as he walked out of the kitchen.

Passing through the hallway, Preston stopped to admire the family pictures. "Why do I do this every time I come over here?" he asked himself as he focused his attention on his father's picture.

"Uh, because you miss him," Donald answered Preston's question as he placed his hand on his shoulder.

Preston nodded his head and glanced at Donald. "Hey, babe, how's the game?"

"I don't know," Donald chuckled. "You know I'm not all that into football. I just watch it cause that's what you are supposed to do on Thanksgiving."

162

"Preston chuckled, "Yeah, basketball is your thing."

"Yup, that's right."

Preston and Donald gazed at the pictures as the family maneuvered around them, all enjoying the day and enjoying each other. They all knew that Preston was attracted to the picture wall, so they paid him no mind.

"So, those were the good ole days, huh?" Donald asked as he admired the photos.

"Yup, the good ole days," Preston replied with a smile. "If only dad could be here right now…" he stopped as he felt his eyes beginning to water.

Thanksgiving was one of the hardest holidays for Preston due to his father dying a week before.

"You know, it's been five years and I still cry when I think of him. I should be over it by now; at least not cry every time."

"Preston, it doesn't matter how much time has passed since your father died. You have the right to mourn him as long as you need to."

Preston wiped a lone tear from his eye and smiled. "Yeah, I guess you're right. You know, I wish he could've met Jordan. I hate that he died a month before he was born."

"Well, look at this way. Jordan was a gift from God that your dad had the pleasure of meeting in heaven," Donald said as he patted Preston's back.

Preston chuckled. "That's a good way to look at it, Don."

"Hey ya'll, mama said come on so we can eat!" Madisyn yelled. "Chad, forget the game and come and eat!" she called out.

"Forget the game?!" Chad exclaimed. "I will never forget about a football game, Maddie."

"Chadbert, come on in here and eat!" Madisyn yelled.

"Chadbert?" Preston frowned and laughed aloud. "What kind of name is Chadbert?"

"Madisyn, I told you about saying my whole government," Chad quipped as he walked past Preston and Donald.

Preston covered his mouth, hoping to contain himself. Failing, he burst out in laughter. Donald chuckled and shook his head.

"What's so funny, *Preston*?" Chad asked in a sarcastic voice. "Your name is crazy too," he said as he walked towards the dining room.

Chad, Preston, and Donald all laughed aloud as they made their way to the dining room.

"Laughing at my name, like your name is all that," Chad continued as he took his seat.

"Oh, hush Chad and get ready to eat this food your baby has cooked," Madisyn said as she gave her boyfriend a quick peck on the lips. "I been in that kitchen for two days."

Preston smiled at his little sister. *I'm glad she found someone to love her and to keep her out of trouble,* he thought to himself as he watched the couple interact.

"Okay everybody, here comes the turkey!" Annie yelled from the kitchen.

A minute later, she walked into the dining room with the turkey in tow.

"Oh, Aunt Annie, that turkey looks so good," Deborah complimented.

"Thank you, sweetie," Annie replied as she sat the turkey down in the middle of the table. "I hope ya'll enjoy it."

"We will!" the family said in unison.

"Oh Lord, I forgot to get the yams!"

"It's okay, Ma. I will go and get them," Madisyn said quickly. "You need to sit down for a while; you've been up cooking since yesterday."

"Thank you, baby," Annie said to her daughter.

"Aunt Annie, you do need to sit down for a while," Deborah commented.

"Yeah, she does," Preston joined with a smile.

"Well, maybe ya'll are right; I do need a little rest."

"Okay, now we can eat!" Madisyn walked into the dining room and sat the candied yams next to its edible counterparts.

"I will say grace this year," Deborah said. "Everybody bow your heads."

"Oh, that's great Deborah," Annie happily complimented as she bowed her head.

"Yeah, Deb, the good Lord would love to hear from you. It's been a while." Madisyn cracked.

"Ha, ha!" Deborah chuckled. "So funny, now hush up and bow your head."

The family laughed as they prepared themselves for Thanksgiving prayer.

"Lord, we thank you," Deborah started but was quickly interrupted by a harsh knock on the front door.

"Who in the world could that be?" Annie looked up, confused.

"Yeah, in all that rain," Chad added.

"I will go and see," Madisyn said as she quickly got up and rushed to the door.

Another harsh bang on the door startled the family, causing Annie to jump.

"Preston! Come on out here and see your son!"

"Oh damn!" Preston groaned as he recognized the troublesome voice.

"What is Stephanie doing here?" Donald asked in an irritated tone.

"I don't know, but I'm sure she's getting ready to mess up our day," Preston huffed.

"Preston! Come on, I don't have all day!" Stephanie yelled.

"Preston, you need to go and handle that girl before I do," Deborah said as she stood up from the table. "Don't make no sense, coming over here startin' mess," Deborah mumbled.

Preston inhaled quickly and exhaled slowly, working to remove the intense pressure that was beginning to form in the middle of his forehead.

"Hi ya'll!" Stephanie emerged from the front of the house and into the dining room and joined the family. "Happy Thanksgiving!"

"You have got to be kidding me," Deborah said slowly.

"How you doing Deb? It's so good to see you."

"You have some nerve. Coming here and acting a fool," Deborah said through clenched teeth.

"I'm just here so my son can see his daddy. I ain't come here to see ya'll," Stephanie quipped.

Why did she let this girl in? Preston asked quietly to himself but kept his mouth closed; careful not to upset the situation further.

"Madisyn, why did you let that thang in here?" Deborah asked, as if she read Preston's mind.

"I didn't! The dummy pushed passed me," Madisyn said as she rolled her eyes.

"You should've knocked her butt out," Deborah replied.

"Yeah, I should've, but my nephew is in the car. I don't want him more scarred than he already is."

"You left my son in the car?" Preston asked, jumping up from his chair.

"Um…yeah… Where else would he be?" Stephanie asked in a sadistic tone. "I mean, he certainly can't come in here," she continued with a devious smirk etched across her face.

Preston quickly moved from the table and pushed passed Stephanie. "You are ridiculous," he mumbled as he walked out of the dining room.

"Look hussy! We are having Thanksgiving dinner and you were not invited. So, I suggest you get up out of here before I put you out!" Deborah yelled.

Grabbing a knife off the turkey's serving platter, Deborah walked closer to Stephanie, pointing it in her face.

Stephanie chuckled. "You better know what to do with that thing," she taunted.

"Deborah, put the knife down," Madisyn pleaded. "You don't want to go out like I did."

"Put it down, Deborah!" Annie joined in, begging her niece.

"Yeah, put it down, Deborah," Stephanie mocked.

"Deb, she ain't worth it," Madisyn said. "Nobody is worth giving up your life. I let my anger get the best of me and now I can't go and do what I want anytime I want because of a stupid mistake. You don't want to be like me Deborah."

"Madisyn, I'm going to take care of this girl once and for all," Deborah said as she raised the knife higher.

The room erupted in panic as Deborah plunged the knife towards Stephanie. Ducking, Stephanie knocked the knife out of Deborah's hand.

"Missed me," she teased with a wicked smile on her face. Deborah smacked Stephanie, knocking her onto the floor.

"I didn't miss you that time, bitch!"

In a flash, Stephanie and Deborah were on the floor, rolling around like two wild cats. Rushing over to the women, Chad grabbed Deborah.

"Get off me!" Stephanie yelled.

"Hey Donald, come and help me, man!" Chad called out as he tried releasing Stephanie from Deborah's death grip. Donald jumped up and sprang into action, working hard to pull the women apart.

"What's going on in here?!" Preston yelled as he ran in, holding his son.

"Jordan, go in the living room for a minute," he quickly said.

"Mommy!" Jordan rang out.

"It's okay, Jordan. Just go into the living room!"

Jordan followed his father's demand and ran out of the dinning room but instead of running into the living room, he ran out the front door.

"Stephanie! What the hell is wrong with you?! Why did you come over here starting shit?!"

169

Chad and Donald were finally able to free Stephanie from Deborah's grip, both exhausted from it all.

"Get the hell out of here and don't come back. And don't even think about taking my son, he's staying here with me." Preston rolled his eyes and walked into the living room. Noticing the door was ajar, he ran to it and called out.

"Jordan?!"

The family all gathered in the living room, with the exception of a pissed off Deborah. She was in the dining room, still in tornado mode.

"Jordan!" Madisyn called out.

Looking over at his mother, Preston noticed that she was clutching her chest right at the same time he heard the sound of what sounded like a firecracker at its peak. In a panic, he ran outside, in a full-fledged mission to find his son.

"Oh God!" Stephanie screamed in a voice full of shrill and devastation.

Preston's stomach dropped in an immense force as he ran to meet Stephanie at her car. At that very moment, his entire existence no longer mattered to him as he saw his five-year-old son with blood pouring from his limp little body as he laid in the passenger seat of his mother's car. His favorite toy fire truck laid beside him on the center armrest and his right hand lightly held a small, black pistol.

170

THE GREGG FAMILY

1

"hy do you have to have the radio so loud?" Sumer Gregg asked her seventeen-year-old brother, Trey.

"It's not loud if I can hear you ask a dumb question," Trey quipped as he slowly approached the red light.

"Okay, I'm going to tell mom and dad," Summer responded as she reached over and turned the volume on the radio down.

"Leave it alone!" Trey yelled. "This is my car and you're lucky that I'm dropping you off at school."

"It's not luck if mom made you do it, jerk."

Ignoring his sister, Trey accelerated slowly through the green light. Bobbing his head to one of his favorite songs, Trey glanced at his cell phone. "Why does this girl text me so early in the morning," he whispered. Picking it up, he quickly typed in his password and proceeded to send a response text to Mariah, his girlfriend of six months.

Aye, I will get at you when I get to school. Meet me at my locker.

Placing his phone back on his lap, Trey slightly shifted his car to the right to allow a dump truck to maneuver its way through the small street that they were both trying to quickly drive on at the same time; both anxious to reach their destinations. Trey was trying to get his sister out of his car as fast as he could, and the driver of the dump truck was undoubtedly trying to get to the construction site that had been taking up space in the neighborhood for an entire year and a half.

"Do you have your lunch money?" Trey asked Summer.

"Yes, I put it in my purse," she answered, smiling brightly.

Trey chuckled, "A purse? Ten years old and you carry a purse," he continued to tease his sister.

"Yup, mommy says all girls should have a purse," Summer boasted.

Hearing the chirp of his phone, Trey looked down at his lap. *Oh, my boy, Justin*, he said silently. Picking his phone up, he quickly read the text.

Yo, you missed a good game last night. Taylor was looking for you.

"Oh word," Trey happily said as he began to type his response. Stopping at the last stop light before he reached his sister's school, he quickly responded to his friend.

I'm going to try to get at her today.

"The light is green," Summer said loudly.

Glancing at his sister, he gave her a side-eyed look and stepped on the gas. Moving forward, he began finishing the text that was interrupted by the green light.

I will talk to you when…

"Trey! Look out!" Summer yelled.

Looking up, Trey saw the minivan, but could do nothing about what was taking place. Swerving, the car went haywire, causing the minivan to run off the road. In a split second, the small red car, carrying Trey and Summer, flipped over and landed in a ditch adjacent to Summer's elementary school.

2

*Y*ou have five minutes to handle your business, Mr. Gregg and then I must be going," Celeste said to her husband, forcing a bothered frown.

"Aw, come on baby. You know I need more time than that."

Celeste smiled at her husband before she entertained his motion for between the sheets action.

"Jason, we both have to get to work. I just got this job and I don't want to mess it up. I've only been there a month. "Besides, I gave in last night. Can't you wait until tonight to do it again?"

"Nope, I can't," he answered quickly. "Come on Celeste, you said after the kids got going, then you would take care of me." Removing his towel, Jason stood naked in front of his wife. "Please?" he begged.

"Agh. Babe, you stay horny. Why are you so horny all the time?"

"Because you got that good-good baby."

Celeste chuckled at her husband; loving the feeling of being wanted. Although she often whined, mainly to give her husband the much-needed chase and hunt that men were always looking for, she basked in the glory of her husband's affection. She was delighted that her husband still found her sexy after two kids, the unsteady ups and downs of life, and twenty-five years of marriage. Unlike most of her friends, she was still happily married with the perfect family and perfect life. So, when her man wanted her, she felt she had no choice but to give in; even when she was at her busiest. She wanted to keep her house intact and her man happy, so sex it was when he wanted it.

"Come on and hurry up! I told you that I have to get to work. We both do," Celeste cried.

"Stop worrying your pretty little head," Jason smiled. "Those nurses can do the work of a nursing assistant, just for a little while," he said nonchalantly. "Let them take a few blood pressures and help a few patients to the bathroom. They ain't doing nothing else."

"Well, you got a point there," she said as she grabbed her husband's man hood and began to massage it.

"Now that's better," Jason moaned as he grabbed his wife's free hand and kissed it gently.

Getting up, Celeste slowly removed her robe and proceeded to follow her husband's nonverbal commands. Finally reaching the bed, Celeste laid down seductively, readying herself for her husband's touch. A faint buzzing sound interrupted Celeste's mood. Stopping her husband just before he entered her, she reached over and grabbed her vibrating phone.

"Really, Celeste? Why are you answering the phone right now?" Jason whined.

"Wait, it's the hospital," she responded. "I know they are going to fire me," she muttered as she sat up and prepared her tone to change into a sick person's voice. "Hello?" She said calmly. Unable to master the voice that she practiced. "Yes, this is Mrs. Gregg." Celeste stood up, listening intently to the caller.

"Who is that, baby?" Jason asked as he noticed the strained look on Celeste's face.

"Oh God! Nooo!" Celeste yelled. "We will be right there!" she screamed before pushing the end button on the phone.

"What is baby? What's wrong?"

"The kids. There's been an accident," she answered in a voice just above a whisper. Grabbing the first article of clothing she saw on the black loveseat across from her bed, she quickly slung it on. A yellow dress that she'd planned to put away in the chess she reserved for all her spring and summer clothes.

"Oh no!" Jason exclaimed. Following his wife's lead, he threw on the sweater and jeans he had planned to wear for the day that he had laid out a few hours earlier. "Are the kids alright?"

Celeste could hear her husband's question, but she could not form the words properly to answer him. A feeling of dread took over her body; one that she surely had never felt before.

"Honey, did they tell you if the kids are alright?"

Mustering up as much energy as she could, she opened her mouth to speak. "Um, they are at the hospital. That's all they could say," she mumbled. "The man just told me to get there as soon as possible."

"Okay, you come on out to the car when you're ready. I will go ahead and get the car warmed up," Jason said quickly while snatching his keys off the dresser.

"He said to go to Glenview Memorial and go straight in the back," Celeste called out to her husband. Fighting back tears, she found a hair tie on the dresser and quickly tied her long black hair into a bun. Not worrying about style, just something to keep the hair out of her face. "No distractions," she said aloud. Walking into the kitchen, Celeste grabbed her wallet and headed out the front door to join her husband, working diligently not to think the worst.

3

*H*ow could I have been so stupid?" Trey questioned, mentally punishing himself as he sat on the hard, grey chair in the hospital's emergency room. He gently massaged his aching, newly casted, left arm with his right hand and sighed. Standing, he started to walk over to the nurses' station but quickly decided against it as the crowd of people seemed to be too busy to answer any of his questions. *What is taking that doctor so long? I thought he said they were almost done with Summer's surgery.* A small group of women walked by and Trey opened his mouth to speak but they quickly walked past him, not bothering to look his way. *Damn, I wish somebody would tell me something.* Feeling hot and a bit flushed, he began to pace back and forth, making sure not to walk too far away from his chair; in case the doctor came out with any news. His mind reverted back to the moment before the accident happened, causing a lone tear to fall down his face. *Damn it... I could've waited to talk to him when I got to school. Why the hell didn't I wait?* Walking back to his chair, he quickly sat down and put his head in his hands.

"Trey!? Oh, thank God!"

Trey looked up at his mother as she rushed over to him, his father close behind.

"What happened son?" his father asked.

"Let me look at you!" Celeste cried as she fumbled with her son's shirt and gently rubbed his casted arm. "Oh my God! What happened? Is it broken?"

"Ma, I'm fine. Just a fracture, that's' all," Trey said quickly as he fought to hold his tears.

"Oh no! My baby." Celeste cried as she continued to gently rub her son's injured arm. "Is anything else broken? Let me see."

"No, just my arm."

"Where is the nurse? Or doctor? Who put the cast on? Did they—"

"What happened?" Jason asked again with a concerned frown etched across his face.

"We were in a car accident. I swear I didn't see the van coming our way. I was driving—"

"Wait a minute," Celeste interrupted. "Where is Summer?!"

Trey looked up at his parents, not sure on how to answer his mother's question.

"Mr. and Mrs. Gregg?"

Celeste and Jason both looked over towards the sound of the voice.

"I'm Doctor Rose. Can we step into the family conference room for a moment? I need to speak with you."

"Um, about what? Where is my daughter?" Celeste asked through a tone above a whisper. "It's never a good sign when a doctor wants to talk to family in the conference room," she commented as she grabbed her husband's hand. Looking over at Trey, she began to cry.

"Trey, where is Summer?"

"Answer your mama boy! Where is your sister?" Jason chimed in.

"Mrs. Gregg, Mr. Gregg, as you probably know, your children were in a car accident. We should go into the conference room to finish our conversation," Dr. Rose said.

"No! I want to see my daughter!" Celeste cried as the tears began to fall faster.

Jason placed his right hand on his wife's shoulder. "Doctor, please tell us what you have to tell us right here. We don't want to go to any conference room."

The doctor looked over at Trey and flashed a sympathetic look. "Mr. and Mrs. Gregg, your daughter sustained life threating injuries. I'm sorry to tell you that your daughter didn't make it. I'm so sincerely sorry," the doctor said before walking away.

4

*A*re you ready to go honey? The family car is here."

"I will be down in a minute, Jason," Celeste replied as she studied her face, a face she didn't recognize in the bathroom mirror. A face gripped with sadness and anger all mixed into one big mess.

"Okay, I will let the director know to go ahead and start loading the other cars," he said softly before walking out of the bathroom.

Standing motionless, she continued to stare at the unfamiliar person staring back at her through the mirror. "How am I supposed to bury my child?" she whispered to herself before a fresh set of tears formed in the corners of her eyes. Her mind continued to fail her as it continued to replay the moment, she saw her lifeless baby girl laying in a cold hospital room. She continued to see her daughter's face, all covered with bruises and her chest riddled with scratches. Her eyes were swollen shut and her mouth was slightly open.

Celeste closed her eyes, hoping to get a break from the horrific image of her daughter's injured, postmortem body but just like all the other times, her mind failed her. No matter how tight she closed her eyes and how hard she tried to get the image to disappear, the vison would always remain.

"Celeste?"

Allowing the tears to flow freely, Celeste turned towards the sound of her mother's voice. "Yes Mama," she answered as she dabbed at her tears.

"Oh baby, how are you holding up?" Lisa asked as she put her arms around her daughter.

"I don't know Mama. I don't think I can do this. I am a strong woman but this…" her voice trailed off as she allowed the tears to continue to fall down her face.

"It's going to be okay baby. This is when we need to let God fight for us," her mother responded as tears began to fall from her eyes. "It's going to be okay."

Celeste allowed herself to become vulnerable, laying her head on her mother's shoulder just as she used to do as a child when she felt the world was closing in on her. "I can't mama. I just can't," she cried as her daughter's mangled body stood front and center in her thoughts.

"Yes, you can baby. We can do this together."

"We tried for months." Celeste started as she lifted her head off her mother's shoulder and stared off in the distance. "You know, Jason was so happy when she was finally here."

"Yes, I remember." Lisa smiled and rubbed her daughter's back.

"You remember when she got a hold of your make-up and daddy got all worried cause he thought she got some in her mouth," Celeste laughed. "Remember that?"

"Yep, we tried to tell your daddy that she was gonna' be alright but he kept right on fussing over her."

Celeste burst out into laughter and smoothed her hair down with her right hand. "Yep, daddy loved himself some Summer."

"Yes, he did baby."

"Now, he can take care of her for me. I hope she's with daddy." Celeste looked up towards the ceiling. "Do you think she made it to Heaven and is with daddy?"

Absolutely baby; they are there together. And I bet Summer is playing with all sorts of makeup, your daddy right with her, making sure she is alright.

Celeste looked at her mother for more reassurance before turning to the mirror and studying her face again. Grabbing a tissue, she wiped her eyes and walked wobbly towards the bathroom door. Holding on to the wall for support, she inhaled deeply and slowly exhaled, a technique the hospital's psychiatrist taught her to do anytime she felt as if she was going to faint. Steadying herself, she grabbed onto her mother's hand as she mentally prepared herself to join her husband and the rest of the family so they could give Summer a farewell fit for a princess.

Trey looked around at the crowd that had gathered in his house after his sister's funeral. "So many people," he hastily muttered as he locked eyes with the principal from Summer's elementary school. "All these years and I still hate that man," he said through clenched teeth. Trey looked stone-faced at Mr. Bird, as the principal gave a sympathetic smile and a wave at him. Choosing not to return the kind gesture, he got up from the couch and moved over to the single chair that sat in the corner. "Maybe I can be alone over here," he griped.

"Hey there son. How are you holding up? You need to go and eat something."

Sighing, he looked up at his Grandma Lisa's brother. "I'm okay, Uncle Andre. I don't have an appetite," he mumbled.

"Yeah, I understand but you need to keep your strength up."

"Maybe later," he quickly responded. *Anything to get this old man away from me*, he silently said to himself. Although he was angry, he still knew not to be blatantly disrespectful.

"Okay, son. I'm going to go and check on your parents. I will be back soon. Okay?"

"Yeah, okay," Trey replied, giving a false smile before his uncle walked away.

Looking over at his mother, Trey's stomach did flips. *I hate to see her cry*, he thought as he held back tears of his own. *Why didn't I just wait until I got to school to start texting? If it wasn't for me, my little sister would still be here, and my mother wouldn't hate me. Now, she's all in some grave way on the other side of town. She is supposed to be here with us. Not lying in some box six feet under.* His mind drifted off to the day at the hospital, when the doctor told his parents what he already knew, that their ten-year-old daughter was dead; all because he was texting and driving. He thought of how his mother fell to her knees as she cried while his father held her. "How could you be so stupid?" he heard his mother cry as she wept. The look of hatred directed towards him crossed his mother's face for the first time ever. *I wish I could erase that look from my mind. My mom now hates me… I don't blame her… I kind of hate myself now.*

Looking out at the crowd, he frowned at them; whishing they would all just go home. Especially his little cousins that were all around the same age as Summer. Watching them reminded him of his sister and it ate away at him. *If Summer was here, she would be running around right along with them.*

Sitting back in the chair, he looked at the huge window that was in the front of the living room; his mother's favorite window and closed his eyes at the family picture that sat directly above it. He could still hear his father's questions as they vividly pierced his memory. *Why Trey? Why would you be texting and driving, son?*" Although his father was more compassionate than his mother, he still knew that deep down inside, his father hated him too for taking his baby girl away from him. *I never seen my father cry, until I killed his daughter*, he said quietly to himself. Not able to contain himself any longer, Trey dropped his head and sobbed.

5

"Wassup, Trey? Sorry about your sister," Stewart, one of Trey's football teammates said as he gave Trey the signature handshake that only friends shared.

"Thanks, man," Trey replied. Standing out at the bus stop, he felt like a stranger. *It's going to be hard riding the bus again after driving to school for a year*, he thought to himself as he watched kids run around like they were still in elementary school instead of the high school students that they were. Pulling the hood of his sweatshirt over his head, he reached in his pocket for his phone. "Where is my phone?" he whispered as he dug deeper into his pocket. "Oh yeah, that's right. They took my phone," he huffed. Looking for something to focus on and pass the time, other than talking with the kids standing around with him, he watched a woman walk by with two small dogs and a man mowing his lawn. No, they weren't interesting to him, he just needed something to push the time and they were it. He watched as one of the dogs squatted to do its business while its owner kept her head on her phone. Looking at the man

193

mowing his lawn he balled his lips at the fact that he reminded him of his father. *I wonder do he have any kids. A daughter?* Sighing, he allowed his mind to go into rant mode as its been doing a lot since his sister's death. Thoughts of his sister calling his name right before they swerved off the road and crashed into the deep ditch that lined the side of the street jumped into his mind and he shook his head; trying desperately to remove it. He heard his sister's voice a lot, especially at night when his mother did her loudest crying and his father paced the floor. Pulling his hood further down, he watched as the school bus slowly approached. "This is going to be a long ass school year," he grumbled as Harriet High and Harriet Middle school's shared bus stopped in front of the kids and extended the long red stop sign. Trey sighed as he waited to get on the bus. Walking onto the bus, he frowned. "Middle schoolers," he muttered while walking all the way to the back, trying to get away from as many people as possible.

"I know you are not going to just walk past me like you don't see me."

Trey looked over to his left to see his girlfriend, Mariah staring up at him. For some reason, he blamed her for all his and his family's misery. *If she didn't text me, then I wouldn't have been looking at my phone when Justin texted*, he told himself on many of his sleepless nights. Sure, he knew it was no way at all her fault, but it helped to temporarily remove the blame off himself.

"Come on, sit here," she said as she patted her seat. Trey obliged and sat down next to her. He didn't want to but at least she was in the back.

"Wassup, Mariah?"

"Nothing just worried about you and your family. How are you guys doing?"

"We good," he lied. *Things went from bad to worst in a matter of days, but she doesn't need to know that*, he silently said to himself.

"You know, Summer's funeral was very touching. So many of her teachers and classmates gave their respects in such a beautiful way," Mariah said with a small smile. "And all the beautiful stuffed animals and flowers were so pretty. My mom said—"

"Yeah," Trey interrupted. I don't want to talk about her funeral," he said, a bit too loudly.

"Oh, sorry, I was just…" Mariah decided not to finish her sentence. Instead, she turned towards the window and looked out.

"I-I'm sorry, Mariah. I just have a lot on my mind. I didn't mean to yell."

"That's okay," Mariah muttered as she continued to look out the window.

Sighing, Trey closed his eyes and tried hard to block out the noise of the overcrowded school bus.

"Trey, can I talk to you for a moment?"

"Why do these teachers keep stopping me? He muttered. Although Ms. Foley, Trey's math teacher was his favorite, he didn't have the mindset to have a conversation with her. "Yes, ma'am," he spoke softly.

"How are you doing? Is there anything I can do for you or your family?"

"No, we are okay."

"Alright, if there is anything that I can do, please let me know. I am going to excuse your test grade; I know math is your favorite subject and it's not like you to fail a test. Under the circumstances, I think it's only right to allow you to retake it in a few weeks. How does that sound?"

"Thank you," he mumbled.

"You're welcome," Ms. Foley said as she tenderly patted Trey on the back. "Go on so you won't be late to your next class," she said as she sat down at her desk.

For effect, he smiled at his teacher before leaving her classroom. Walking out into the hall, Trey maneuvered as quickly as he could to his locker, trying his best to avoid more teachers. "They been stopping me all day," he mumbled as he pulled his hood over his head and quickly removed it as it was a school rule not to have it on during school hours. His teachers had been paying so much attention to him since he's been back that they would for sure notice it. Unlike all the other times he popped his hoodie on his head, and they paid him nor his friends any mind. They just wanted to get the day started and ending as fast as they possibly could. Now, it was like they were all on a mission to keep their eyes on him; to make sure he didn't go into some sort of mental breakdown. Finally reaching his locker, Trey threw his book bag on the floor.

"Hi Trey," Twila, one of Mariah's frenemies said as she stood at her locker next to Trey's.

"Wassup Twila?" Trey spoke as he fumbled with his locker. "Shouldn't your locker be in the eleventh-grade hall?" He asked.

"Yes, it's supposed to be, but I was having some problems with it. The door is jammed so they moved me to the twelve-grade hall. It was the only available one for now," she explained as she rumbled through the contents of the locker. "How are you doing?" She asked

"If one more person asks me how I'm doing," he mumbled to himself. "I'm good."

"I remember when I used to babysit Summer," Twila said as she looked off in the distance. "She was a good kid; never caused any trouble."

Not wanting to snap at Twila like he snapped at Mariah earlier, he kept quiet; allowing Twila to reminisce. *She did babysit Summer for my parents anytime they needed her to; anytime I couldn't do it due to football practice. I'm sure she's grieving too.*

"I am going to miss her like crazy," Twila said as she began to cry.

"Yeah, I know," Trey said as genuinely as he could. Feeling himself getting frustrated, he closed his locker and threw his book bag over his shoulder. "I better get to class. See you later Twila."

"See ya," Twila said as she wiped away tears with the back of her hand.

Trey sighed. "So tired of everybody crying," he muttered as he walked towards his social studies class.

6

"ow does Chinese sound for tonight?"

Celeste looked at her husband like he was crazy. "Food? Are you kidding me? You know I don't want anything to eat!" she snapped.

"Come one Celeste," the doctor said you need to eat, Jason pleaded. "It's not healthy for you to continue to starve yourself."

"If my baby can't eat, then I won't eat. Period!"

Jason sat down on the loveseat next to his wife. "Celeste, I know this is hard for you. It's hard for all of us to know that our daughter is never coming home again, but we have to find a way to start putting our lives back in order. Of course, slowly but we have to do it, honey. You know, Trey and I—"

"Don't say his name," Celeste harshly cut in. "I don't want to talk about him."

Celeste hated the way she now felt about her son, her first born but she couldn't help herself. The mention of her son's name brought a hard, devasting cringe to her body so she avoided his name and him at all cost. The sound of it physically made her sick and she hated herself for it.

199

"Please don't bring his name up in front of me again," she said to her husband. Not really believing her own words. *How can I feel so much hatred for my own son?* She thought quietly.

He took your daughter away from you; that's why, the tiny voice that had been speaking to her since her daughter's death lectured loudly to her, almost yelling at her. *How could you ever love that boy again?* The voice roared.

"Celeste, he's our son. How could you be so cruel?" Jason asked in a voice that wasn't his own. "He's hurting too."

"Yeah, well, if it wasn't for our *son*, this mess wouldn't be happening. I would be taking my daughter to her ballet class right now instead of sitting here holding her picture. If it wasn't for *Trey*, I wouldn't have to go to a freakin' graveyard every day!"

"Celeste?"

"Jason, just stop! Okay? I'm in no mood to continue this conversation. If that boy wasn't texting while he was driving, then none of this would be happening."

Jason remained quiet as his wife vented her frustration.

"I mean, what was so important that he couldn't wait? The boy just had to pull out that stupid phone." Celeste stood up and began pacing, holding Summer's picture against her chest. "And then, we now have court dates. I've never been sued for anything before. Now the driver of the minivan is suing us. You know that man is now paralyzed because of that boy's negligence?!"

"Trey, Celeste! The boy's name is Trey and he made a mistake!" Jason yelled. "You are his mother," he said a bit more calmly. "Trey needs us, Celeste."

Celeste looked up at the ceiling, refusing to speak.

"Okay, if you can't love him, then I will do it for the both of us!" Jason spat as he got up and walked out the front door; slamming it hard behind him.

Celeste kept her eyes on the door for a minute longer before she flopped down on the couch and pulled her knees up to her chest. Her eyes began to burn and a feeling of butterflies fluttering began to take place in the pit of her stomach. She looked down at the picture she was holding and smiled. A picture that was taken at a much happier time in life; when her and her family had the life that all the people around her wanted. The picture reminded her of her life when it was all intact and picture perfect. She smiled at the pink and purple barrettes that hung on each of her daughter's braids and the necklace that graced her neck and sat loosely on her shirt. "So pretty", she mumbled before readjusting herself on the couch. Pulling the picture close to her chest again, she laid her head on one of the decorative pillows and closed her eyes. As usual, thoughts of her daughter covered her mind from top to bottom, from left to right and she smiled. Grateful that this time, they were happy

201

thoughts and not the grisly ones that usually visited her at night. She smiled as she watched Summer dance around the house and sang as loud as she could to her favorite song, Beyoncé's, Run the World. "My baby," she said aloud as she watched Summer try her hardest to dance and move around like Beyoncé. Celeste opened her eyes and looked towards the front door again before her mind could take a cruel turn and move in the direction of the nightly thoughts. It's been known to do it and she was determined to beat her thoughts at its own game. "I'm going crazy," she whispered as she sat up on the couch and stretched before slowly sliding down to the floor. "How am I going to live my life without her?" Moving her right hand over her eyes, she wiped away tears before lying on her back. She stared at the ceiling for a few seconds before surveying the rest of her living room, smiling at each picture that had Summer's face attached to it. Shutting her eyes again, she cradled Summer's picture as she waited for the thoughts to begin. Hoping for the good ones, she allowed her mind to overtake her. Propping her feet on the couch, she relaxed her muscles, preparing herself for another round of memories.

Jason watched his son from a distance. "The poor kid," he mumbled and shook his head. "I know he is messed up about all this and I don't know what to do to help him." Leaning against the side of the house, Jason continued to painfully watch his son; watched the pain and the sadness in his eyes that had replaced the rambunctious and cheerful glee that was previously in them before the fateful accident. He missed the charismatic football player that all the girls adored and the smile that reminded him of his younger days. Jason wanted his son back; the same son he had before all the problems. An image of Summer popped into his mind, causing him to smile. "Daddy misses you baby," he whispered. Knowing that his wife had thoughts of their daughter on lock, he forced his thoughts of her out of his mind, choosing to focus on his son.

"Hey son, whatcha doing?" Jason cheerfully said as he entered into the garage.

Jason knew that Trey was tired of everyone asking him *how* he was doing so he stuck with whatcha doing.

"Hey dad, just fixing my bike."

"I didn't know your bike was broken," Jason smiled as he pulled his toolbox off the shelf and sat it down next to his son.

There was a pause before either of them spoke. Jason knew that Trey wasn't going to say anything, and he scrambled to think of something to say that wouldn't bring either of them to more sadness.

"Uh, you know," he started as he gazed around in "dad mode" at the contents in the garage. "This garage sure could use a good cleaning. Whatchu think?"

Trey kept his eyes on the task at hand, not bothering to look up at his dad. "Yeah," he somberly replied.

Jason frowned, hating to see his so in so much pain. *Normally, when I mention cleaning the garage, Trey gives a huge protest on why we shouldn't,* he though quietly, desperately wanting his son back. Thinking of more to say, Jason lightly bit his lower lip. "You know, when I was a kid, I didn't know anything about fixing bikes. I didn't know about fixing anything for that matter," he chuckled, hoping that another approach would work. "You have a gift son," he smiled at Trey, hoping that the compliment would bring him out of his funk.

Trey continued to look down at his bike, not paying his father any attention.

"Listen Trey…" he started but stopped to give his mind time to catch up. At this point, small talk wasn't going to work, and he needed something more profound to say.

Moving the wheel of the bike forward, Trey maneuvered just enough to give his bike renewed attention by focusing on another part.

"Look at me, son."

Trey reluctantly lifted his head.

"Listen…I- I know you feel bad about what happened." He stopped himself and thought about his words carefully before he continued. "We all do but you have to find a way to get past…well, not get past but find a way to get through life. We can't bring your sister back son, no matter how much we mope around."

"Yeah well, if it wasn't for me, she would still be here."

Jason tilted his head towards the sky as he again searched his brain for more answers.

"Trey stop it. That's enough of you throwing blame on yourself. Yes, we know you were texting while driving. We know that, so it's no need to continue to tell that story." Taking a minute to inhale a calming breath, Jason went further, trying his hardest to bring his son out of his misery. "Son, I love you and I'm going to see you through this. Me, you…, and your mom will get through this together."

"Mom hates me, Dad. I didn't mean to kill…" Trey stopped, pushed his bike down on the ground, and put his head in his hands.

"Come here son," Jason pulled his son close to him and hugged him tight. "Your mama doesn't hate you; she's just hurting." Jason's heart broke all over again, but this time for his son; hearing his son cry took a toll on him. "It's ok son, let it all out. Go ahead and get it out son, that's right. Let it go," Jason soothed.

As Jason consoled his son, a lone tear fell from his eye. At that moment, he knew that he had a long journey ahead of him. The road to recovery had just begun.

7

*T*rey gazed blankly out the big rectangular window as the bus drove its normal slow drive through the neighborhood. He closed his eyes at the sound of his girlfriend's voice not wanting to be bothered with her or with anyone for that matter. He dreaded each and every school day and hated that his dad forced him to go even when he told him that he didn't feel well. Through Mariah's constant talking, he heard his father's voice. *School is important son; you can't get anywhere in this world without an education. The world doesn't care if you are sick so I can't allow you to use that as an excuse. If you don't have a fever or nothing like that, then you're going.* The noise from the bus alone made him sick and he wanted to be anywhere but there. Looking down at his cast, he frowned. The itching from his healing arm was driving him nuts and there was nothing he could do about it, which made his days coupled with the noisy kids almost unbearable.

"I think I'm going to wear purple. I still gotta' get my hair and my nails done before I can do anything else," Mariah continued on with her one-sided conversation.

I wish she was shut up. Looking at Mariah, he kept his face blank, hoping that his silence would be an indication that he wanted her to be quiet and to leave him alone. As always, she smiled politely at him, grabbed his hand, and kept on talking.

"I was thinking I could go after the game, but I don't think I'll make it over there in time. That nail shop be mad crowded on Fridays."

Having the slightest idea on what Mariah was talking about, Trey turned his back towards the window, pretended to pay attention to Mariah's chat, and waited for the long dreadful ride to be over.

"How's your arm feeling? You haven't said anything about it since it's been broken."

Although Trey was tired of hearing Mariah ramble, he was glad that someone still cared about him. His life at home was in shambles due to the fact that his mother didn't say a word to him; not even a hello. His father, well he was around for him, but Trey couldn't help but to think that he too hated him because of the accident. The only person he felt truly cared about him at this point was his girlfriend and maybe is grandmother. He was still trying to figure that out.

"It's cool," he mumbled.

Sitting across from Mariah, he did his best to show her some attention. Besides, he had to at least act like he cared about what she was talking about. If he was going to keep some sort of support, he had to pretend to be engaged.

"That's good. My mom said you shouldn't scratch or pick at it or anything. You should let it heal."

Trey chuckled, "I can't even if I wanted to. The doctor got my arm on lock so I can't pick at it," he lifted his arm and smiled.

Mariah giggled. "Yeah, that's true."

Surveying his surroundings, Trey slightly shook his head at the crowds that formed in the cafeteria. Some were standing around laughing and conversing while others were quietly eating their lunch. He looked down at his tray before pushing it off to the side.

"What's wrong? Not hungry?" Mariah popped a potato chip in her mouth and readjusted herself in her seat.

"You know I don't eat this shit," he mumbled.

"Yeah, Mariah said as she pulled another chip out of the bag and nibbled on it. "You want some chips?" She offered.

"Nah, I'm good. I'll eat when I get home."

Putting his head down, he ignored the growling from his stomach and itching from his arm. It wasn't like him to not have anything for lunch, even if it was just a bag of chips and some flavored water. His mother always gave him lunch money so he wouldn't have to rely on whatever Harriet High School had to offer for the day. Harriet High was a good school, but they weren't known for their "great cuisine". Most kids hated to eat the lunch, so his mother gave him a few dollars every morning. On the other hand, his father thought he should eat whatever the school offered for lunch. He believed that Trey should learn to appreciate what's offered as some kids didn't have anything at all to eat. To keep the peace in the Gregg household, the morning payday was a secret that only Trey and his mom shared. Now, he and his mom didn't share that or anything else for that matter. Trey felt like a stranger in his own home, a home he once knew he could go to and would always feel loved, welcomed, wanted, protected, and safe. Now, he loathed at the thought of going home but that was the only place he could go. His car was destroyed in the accident and he had no money, so his house was the only place accessible. Sighing, Trey lifted his head and slightly patted his casted arm.

"You sure you don't want some chips? Or at least something to drink? I got a dollar if you want it."

Trey looked at Mariah and smiled. "Nah, I'm good."

"Hey girl! You going to practice today?"

210

"Dang! You scared me!" Mariah cried out and held her chest. "Where did you come from?" She said loudly to her best friend, Casey.

"I just got here. Ms. Brooks held me hostage until I finished the quiz."

"Hey Trey."

"Sup," Trey mumbled and looked down at his arm.

"Are you going?"

"Going where?" Mariah frowned as she ate the last of her chips.

"Practice!"

"Girl, have anybody ever told you that you are too loud and overbearing?"

"Yep, you!" Casey laughed.

Mariah shook her head and threw her empty bag on the table.

"So, Trey…"

Trey looked up at Casey and waited for her to say something, most likely something disrespectful. Although she didn't mean to be, she was sort of on the rude side; one of those ones who had no filter and would say or ask just about anything.

"Your parents still mad at you for—"

"Casey!" Mariah sharply interrupted and shook her head.

"What?!"

"Don't worry about my people! None of your business!"

"Damn, I was just asking."

"And you didn't have to cut me off," Casey nudged Mariah, stood up, and stormed off.

Trey kept his eyes fixed on Casey as she walked towards a group of boys, stopping to talk to her brother.

Sighing, Trey stood up as he knew exactly what was going on and Casey's main reason for storming off. It wasn't that she was upset, it was all about getting some trouble started; something she was known for doing. Casey pointed at Trey and smirked. Deciding not to wait for the trouble to come to him, Trey walked over to Casey and her brother, Dontae.

"Yo, you better watch how you talk to my sister. You already know what it is."

"So! Trey yelled. Ain't nobody scared of you or yo' homies."

"Trey come on." Mariah pleaded while gently pulling Trey's arm.

Trey looked back at Mariah and then back at Dontae. The group of boys with Dontae all stepped forward to confront Trey.

"Oh, so it takes all ya'll for one person?!" Mariah yelled and stood in front of Trey.

"Mariah, go over there. Ain't nobody scared of them."

"Keep talking boy and I'ma put a cast on the other arm."

In an instant, Trey punched Dontae in the mouth with his free hand, knocking him to the floor.

"Damnnnn! He knocked him out… and with a cast on his arm!" One of the kids yelled out behind him while another group of kids laughed.

Trey looked behind him to see the usual spectators gathered around and the two teachers who were on lunch duty running towards him.

"Why Trey?!" Mariah yelled and quickly walked away while Casey kneeled down to the floor, trying to wake her brother. Surprised at how hard he was able to hit Dontae with his non-dominate hand, Trey slowly walked backwards right before Mr. Stokes grabbed him.

"To the office!" Mr. Stokes yelled loudly while the other gym teacher called for help on his walkie talkie.

Pulling himself out of Mr. Stokes' grip, Trey walked out of the cafeteria and to the office, not bothering to look back at the scene he'd caused. His main concern was how his father would take the news of what he did. As he walked, he hoped that his father wouldn't take his mother's lead and abandon him too.

8

*T*hat feels good," Celeste breathed a sigh of release. "A foot massage is just what I need today."

"Good; I'm glad you like it," Jason said as he grabbed more massage oil and slowly rubbed it on his wife's left foot.

"Yes, I do," Celeste smiled.

Jason was glad to see his wife smile. Although she still held Summer's picture close to her all day, every day, he saw improvement in her mood. *Maybe this is a good time to ease Trey's name into the conversation*, he thought. *I am going to fix my family*, he said to himself before going forward with bringing his son's name into the mix. "You know, Trey has a game coming up on Friday." He waited for a response from Celeste before he continued. Looking at his wife, he saw no emotion. *It's certainly better than seeing a frown*. Deciding to continue, he went further. "I think we should go. We should be there to—"

"I'll think about it," Celeste interrupted.

"Okay, alright," Jason smiled, his voice full of relief.

Feeling his phone vibrate in his pocket, Jason reached in and pulled it out. "The school is calling," he mumbled.

"Hello? Yeah, this is Mr. Gregg. Oh yes, Ms. Bryant. How are you?

Jason looked over at his wife and smiled lightly while listening to the school's guidance counselor.

"Oh, I see. Okay, I will be right there. Thanks for calling."

Clicking off his phone, Jason shook his head and stood up. "That was Ms. Bryant. Trey has gotten into a fight this afternoon. I got to go and pick him up, do you want to come with me?"

Celeste looked at Jason as if he had two sets of eyes.

"Okay, I will go alone," he said as he leaned down and kissed his wife on the forehead. I will be back in a little while.

"What were you thinking? You know if you're suspended from school, then you're suspended from playing football?"

Trey sat quietly, watching the trees quickly whip by as his father drove.

"Trey?"

"I don't know Dad," Trey sighed. "If he wasn't running his mouth, then I wouldn't have hit him."

"So, you hit him first?"

Trey continued to look out the window.

"You know you're not supposed to—"

"Put my hands on somebody. I know Dad," Trey interrupted. "But if he would've just minded his own business, none of this would've happened."

"Well, what exactly did he say to get you all riled up?"

Trey kept his eyes on the scenery outside before he answered his father's question. "His sister started it; something about sister-killer and some other stuff she was talking. Then Dontae jumped in it, so I punched him in his mouth." Trey omitted the part where he stood up first, knowing that if he'd told the entire truth, then his father would have a good reason to blame him and he couldn't have that. So, he stuck to the story he'd rehearsed while sitting in the principal's office.

"Son, now you know better than that. You can't go around knocking people out because you don't like the conversation. Why didn't you just walk away?"

Trey sighed and closed his eyes, all the while keeping his head turned away from his father. "I should've," he said but kept his eyes closed, hoping that his standoffish demeanor would somehow stop his father from asking questions. For

217

added effect, he pulled his hoodie over his head, forcing the conversation with his dad to end.

9

hy would he send me flowers?" Celeste huffed under her breath. "I've seen enough flowers at the funeral to last me a lifetime," she continued as she placed the grocery bags on the kitchen counter. "Can't knock my husband for trying though." Looking at the pile of mail she placed on the counter days prior, Celeste sighed. "Nothing but bills I bet," she said as she picked up the stack and threw them all in the trash. "I'm sure there's one from the lawyer's office somewhere in there too," she quipped as she walked over to the refrigerator. A loud bang interrupted Celeste's action. "What was that?" she whispered. Listening closer, she realized it was coming from the backyard. Walking over to the window, she spotted her son throwing a basketball forcefully at the garage door. "Hmph, I should've known," she mumbled. "That boy should be in school instead of messing up my garage door."

"Celeste?"

Celeste turned to see her mother standing in the living room.

"Mama, how did you—"

"The door was wide open. You know better than to leave your door open like that. I'm glad I came over instead of some maniac."

"How you are doing Mama?" Celeste asked as she pulled a chair from the kitchen table and sat down.

"I'm good baby, but the question is, how are you doing?"

Celeste combed her right hand through her hair, "I don't know Mama. Some days I'm okay and others I feel like I am dying." Grabbing the saltshaker from the middle of the table, she moved it around slowly and laid her head on the table.

"Yeah, but it will get better. You just watch and see."

Giving her mother a small smile, Celeste kept her head down and continued to playfully nudge the contents on her table.

"How's Trey handling all this?"

Celeste looked away from her mother and focused her eyes towards the window as she gathered her thoughts on how exactly to answer the question without raising her mother's eyebrows. "He's fine, I guess."

"Guess? What do you mean you guess?"

Celeste lifted her head off the table an looked out at her son. *I can't tell my mother that I hate my own child. Well, it is his fault that I am suffering. Maybe Mama would understand,* she thought quietly before responding to her mother. "I just stay away from him," she started. "I-I mean, he is the reason why my daughter is buried in the ground and not here with me."

Celeste looked at her mother in search for comfort, perhaps, even a little guidance. Finding nothing she was hoping for, Celeste turned away form the shocked and bewildered look that she found instead.

"Celeste, chile, what is the matter with you? Trey is your child too and he needs you. What do you mean you just stay away from him?"

Sighing Celeste leaned back in her seat and rubbed her left temple. "I-I can't face him Ma; I just can't." Tears began to form in the creases of Celeste's eyes for the fifth time in one day. *No more tears*, she coached herself as she wiped them from her face. Celeste looked at her mother and this time, was hoping to see understanding. Instead, she saw a woman who was confused out of her mind.

"I can't believe you, Celeste. That boy needs his mama, especially now!"

Celeste nodded her head and kept her eyes on her mother.

"You get your son and you hug him, hold him. Tell him that you care about his feelings."

"So, I need to lie to him? Is that it mama? I do not like him, and I don't care!"

"Girl, I should smack you right now! You just don't know how blessed you are."

Celeste remained quiet as her mother spoke, not really paying attention to her rant. Her mind was made up and nobody, not even her mother, was going to change it.

"Let me ask you this, what is Jason doing? Has he abandoned Trey too?"

Celeste sighed, "Nope, he spends lots of time with him."

"Well, thank the good Lord that one of his parents still has some sense. You are not doing right, girl. Now I know you miss Summer. We all do, but you can't just let Trey fend for himself. He needs us, all of us. Is that him I hear out there?" Getting up from the table, Lisa walked to the window and peered out. "I'm going to go and talk to him," she informed her daughter as she opened the back door and stormed out.

"Humph, didn't think she would get mad at me," Celeste muttered. "A little support, you would think."

Yeah, that's how Trey feels. He needs a little support from his mother, her inner voice spoke to her. "Whatever!" she blurted out. "I can feel how I want to feel," she huffed while getting up from the table and walking towards the stairs. "Sleep always helps," she said aloud while stomping up the stairs.

10

*Y*eah, my dad just bought me this car. How ya'll like it?"

"It's cray, man. I know you are glad your parents let you drive again."

"Yeah, Stewart, I was getting tired of riding a bike around. It was getting old real quick," Trey beamed.

"I know! It was crazy seeing you ride around on your bike instead of driving," Jeremy, another one of Trey's and Stewart's teammates said.

"Anyway," Trey replied, "those days are over. Back to driving wherever I need to go. So, Jeremy, wassup with Angel?"

"Angel? Trey, did you forget that you have a crazy girlfriend. Mariah is crazy, yo! You know how she got into that fight with Bianca because you were talking to her in the hallway. The crazy thing is, you was trying to get her number for me!"

"Yeah, Mariah is crazy," Trey chuckled. "That's why I'm asking about Angel. Time to switch it up."

"No, I think you need to just deal with Mariah," Stewart jumped in. "You don't want the mess I had to deal with when I was talking to Ebony and Michelle at the same time. It's hard keeping those females away from each other."

"Yeah, but you didn't know what you was doing. I will be able to handle my females," Trey said as he turned the music up.

"Whateva, man," Stewart responded.

"What time is practice today?" Trey asked, ready to change the subject.

"I think coach said at five; he had something to take care of," Jeremy answered.

"Okay, then we have some time to get to…"

Boom! The car smacked into a guard rail, causing the teenagers to cry out.

"No, not again!" Trey yelled.

"Man, what did you do?!" Jeremy yelled.

"I don't know, I was just…" Trey's words trailed off as he noticed that the car was leaning against the guard rail and hanging off the edge of a hill.

"Damn Trey! What is wrong with you?!" Stewart called out, terrified.

"Shut up! Just shut up! We are getting ready to fall. We need to figure out how to get out!" Jeremy nervously shouted.

Trey closed his eyes and thought of his mother. *Maybe this will make her happy*, he thought. *If I die today, she can finally have her justice.* A loud knocking sound pushed Trey out of his thoughts of his mother. "What's that?" He whispered.

"Jeremy?! Stewart?!" Trey called out and looked around. To his surprise, his friends were gone. "What the...?" his voice trailed off. Another pounding sound came from the roof of the car, this time sounding like a bout of thunder.

"Trey!" He heard his father call. "Jeremy?! Stewart?!"

"Trey, open up the door!"

In an instant, Trey was staring at the door to his bedroom, balled up in a corner.

"Dad?!" He yelled.

"Yeah son, why were you yelling? Are your friends in there with you? I heard you yelling Jeremy and Stewart's names! Open up this door before I break it down!"

Jumping up to his feet, Trey ran to the door, unlocked it and stood back, waiting for his father to appear.

"Trey! Are you alright, son?"

"Um, I-I, um."

"Trey talk to me. What's going on?"

Trey sat down on his bed. *If I tell him what goes through my mind, he will think I'm crazy. Well, he has always had my back, maybe he will have my back on this too.*

"Trey?"

"Well dad," he began and looked up at his father, "I've been having thoughts going through my mind."

"Thoughts? What kind of thoughts?"

"Really bad thoughts," he responded shyly. "It's like my mind takes me somewhere; sometimes I'm in danger and other times, I'm not."

"Son? I don't understand. What are you talking about?"

Trey shook his head, trying to clear the memory of what just happened minutes before. "My mind takes me places. Like today, I was in a car with Jeremy and Stewart and we were in an accident. I was driving, and I hit one of those rails that hang on the side of the street. Next thing I knew, we were dangling off the side of a big hill, getting ready to fall. The guys disappeared and then I heard you calling my name."

Trey looked over at his dad and saw that he had tears in his eyes.

"Okay," his father said. "Okay son, I think it's time to call for help. You haven't been yourself since—"

"Since I killed Sumer; I know dad."

"No, that's not what I was going to say. You stop saying that. I don't want you saying that you killed your sister. It was an accident and unfortunately—"

"I killed Summer."

"That's enough, Trey! I said stop!"

Trey put his head down in his hands.

226

"Son, you said that your mind takes you places. Where else has it taken you?"

Trey looked up and focused his mind on his basketball net. "Just small places. Like sometimes, I will be in the kitchen at first and then I will be outside and then back in the kitchen again. This is the first time I was in a car… getting ready to die. It's never been this scary before. This is the first time it seemed like I was going to die. Then, there was one time that a dog was chasing me, but I was able to run fast enough to get away from it."

Jason shook his head. "Yeah, it's time to get some help; some family counseling and a doctor. Son, I'm going to go and make some phone calls. I'll be back in a minute. Will you be okay while I do that?"

"Yeah dad, I'll be fine. I am fine," he said and smiled, hoping to give his dad some reassurance.

"Alright, I will be right back," his father smiled back at him.

Laying back on his bed, Trey thought of the wild thoughts that often went through his mind. *Why is this happening to me?* He asked himself. The buzzing of his cellphone interrupted his mind from going haywire on all the "why me" thoughts.

Hey Trey…wyd?

"Not now Mariah," he whispered before typing a response.

Chillin…

Are you coming outside today?

"I don't feel like going nowhere," he mumbled.

No

Okay...

"What? I can't believe she's not going crazy because I don't want to go outside," he said aloud.

Sighing heavily, he got up and looked out his bedroom window. Rubbing the curtains with his left hand, he frowned. "I wish things can get back to normal," he whispered. "I wish there was a way to fix all this." Grabbing his football, he flopped back down on his bed and began tossing it lightly in the air. "I got to fix this," he mumbled.

"Yeah, um, my name is Jason Gregg and I was calling to set up an appointment.... Yes, family counseling.... Yes, I have private insurance...Okay, I can bring my insurance card with me when I come in...Is there a co-payment? Okay, great, thank you. I will bring all the necessary paperwork with me as well as my insurance information on.... what day did you say? Right, Thursday at nine. My family and I will be there. Thanks so much, see you on Thursday."

Hanging up the phone, Jason sighed loudly. "I have to get my family back on track. My wife is not talking to our son. My son is suffering from some sort of mental breakdown. All this is a mess and I am going to get things moving in a positive direction." Looking down at the information he'd written down from his phone conversation, he smiled. "Hold on family, I got us," he mumbled before heading back upstairs to check on his son.

"I don't know why I haven't thought of this before." Getting up from his bed and throwing his football on the floor, Trey walked towards his door and opened it slowly. Looking around in the hall, he walked out cautiously. "I think he keeps it in the hall closet," he muttered. Looking towards the stairs, he quietly walked closer to the closet, careful not to make any noise. "I don't want to wake her up," he mumbled as he slowly pulled open the closet door. Looking back once more, he noticed that the hall was still quiet, so he swiftly reached for the top shelf and pulled down the black box that lay hidden under his mother's favorite towels. Grabbing it tightly, he walked quickly to his room and closed the door. Sitting down on his bed, he stared at the box, contemplating his next move.

"Trey?"

Shoving the box under his bed with his right foot, he looked towards the door. "Yeah, dad?"

"Are you alright, son?"

"Uh, yeah, come in."

Trey continued to keep his eyes focused on the door and his right heel on the black box.

"Okay, I'm just checking in on you. I called a therapist. We will all go together on Thursday."

"Okay, dad," Trey replied. "Sounds good. Whatever helps," he added.

"Uh, okay, alright. Sounds good to me too son. We need to get this family back on track."

"Yeah. Hey dad, are your keys downstairs on the rack? I need to grab my history book out of your car."

"Your history book? What is—"

"I left it in there the other day while I was studying. I was looking for a quiet place to study for my test and your car won," Trey replied with a smile. He knew the story sounded ridiculous, but he figured his dad would buy anything at this point due to his concern.

"Well, okay, they are downstairs. I'm going to go and check on your mom. She's been sleeping most of the day."

"Yeah," Trey said.

"Alright, see you in a little while. Maybe we will go out to dinner later. How does that sound?"

"Sounds good, Pop."

"Okay, I will let you know when I'm ready."

"Alright," Trey said and smiled with emphasis.

Trey waited patiently as his father walked out of his bedroom and closed the door behind him.

"You know you've been laying in this bed all day," Jason said to his wife as he kissed her on the forehead. "It's time to get up and mingle."

"I just don't have the energy to move around," Celeste replied.

"Yeah, well, you should force yourself to move around. Maybe go out and get some fresh air."

There was a silence before Jason continued.

"How about calling your mother—"

"No, I said I was good. I don't want to go out and do anything. I just want to stay in bed and rest," Celeste forcefully interjected.

"Okay, all right, whatever you want to do. I just thought…"

"Yes, I know what you thought and thank you for your concern but I'm good right where I am."

Getting up slowly off his bed, Jason shook his head and walked towards the door. Turning, he opened his mouth to speak but quickly decided against it. Instead, he walked out into the hall, closing the bedroom door behind him. Sighing, he maneuvered towards the stairs but was stopped in his tracks. Listening closely, he heard his son saying something, but he couldn't quite make out what was being said. *Maybe I should go in there and check on him*, he thought to himself. Walking to his son's bedroom door, he tapped on it softly. "Trey? Everything okay?" Waiting a few seconds for a response, he pushed his ear to the door and heard some muffled cries. Barging in, he saw the worst scene of his life.

"Trey! What are you doing?! Put it down!"

"No dad! I have to do this!"

Jason watched helplessly as his son held a black pistol, his pistol, to the side of his head.

"Trey, please son. We can work through whatever problems you are having. Killing yourself is not the way. Put the gun down, son," Jason pleaded.

"No dad, I don't want to be here anymore. I will give mom what she wants. I will make her happy again by getting rid of the person who took her baby away from her. I need to do this dad, so I can fix things for the family. I will always be around to check on you, just not in human form."

Jason had never heard his son talk like this and for sure never heard of him contemplating suicide.

"I promise we will work through all this. Me, you, and your mom. Your mom doesn't want you to leave; she's just grieving. Soon, she will be back to normal and we can have a happy family again. Son, you have to trust me."

"I'm sorry Dad," Trey said in a whisper as he pulled the trigger.

Yolanda's Note

Hello Loves!

I hope you enjoyed the introduction to each story line and that you are craving for more. I want to give you a taste of each family and their messes before their full stories are released!

Amanda…

Amanda and her twisted baby daddy and his equally deranged mother. What happens after the shot goes off? Did anybody die? Was anyone wounded and if so, was it a foe or a friend?

Preston…

Preston went through hell and back with his relationships. There is Stephanie, not bothering to pay him any mind and respect his relationship with Donald and Donald with his jealousy and frequent outrages and outbursts. What is a man to do? What happens after the family runs out to Stephanie's car after she interrupts their Thanksgiving dinner? Does Donald

235

have reason to worry about Stephanie? They say, tragedy can sometimes bring people closer together, but what about them?

The Greggs...

Celeste, Jason, and Trey went through a lot of mental trauma and anguish following the tragic loss of Summer. Celeste's grief alone causes her entire family unit to fall, Trey feels helpless and desperately wants his mother's love again, and Jason, his father, is stuck in the middle. Will the Greggs mend their family after so much pain and become strong again? Will Celeste reach out to her son and comfort him or will she turn her back against him and their family?

Love,

Yolanda

Meet the Author!

Yolanda Randolph is the creator of the **#Her Intuition Movement**, a movement dedicated to empowering and motivating women to be at their best and to remind them of their worth. Yolanda is also a Credentialed Medical Coder, mother of three teenagers and the owner of Madisyn, her beloved Yorkshire terrier.

Yolanda is an avid reader and loves to write as well. She is dedicated to helping young women reach their highest potential through telling her stories. A survivor of domestic violence and many trials throughout her life, she has become persistent with encouraging others; in hopes that she is an inspiration.

Originally from Baltimore, Maryland, Yolanda now lives in Greenville, NC with her family.

STAY CONNECTED WITH YOLANDA

- **Facebook-** *Yolanda Randolph Publications*
- **Instagram-** *Yolanda Randolph*
- **Twitter-** *YolandaRWrites*
- **Website-** www.yolandarandolph.com
- *Pink Roses* on Facebook and Instagram (A teen community)